THE RADIO RED KILLER

Veteran broadcaster 'Radio Red' Bob Bjorner is the last of the red-hot lefties working at radio station KRED in Berkeley. His paranoia makes him lock his studio against intruders while he's on the air — but his precaution doesn't save him from a horrible death that leaves him slumped at the microphone just before his three o'clock daily broadcast. Homicide detective Marvia Plum scrambles to the station to investigate. Who amongst the broadcasters, engineers, and administrators present at the station was the murderer — and why?

RICHARD A. LUPOFF

THE RADIO RED KILLER

Complete and Unabridged

LINFORD
Leicester

First published in Great Britain

First Linford Edition
published 2016

A catalogue record for this book is available
from the British Library.

ISBN 978–1–4448–3095–8

Published by
F. A. Thorpe (Publishing)
Anstey, Leicestershire
Set by Words & Graphics Ltd.
Anstey, Leicestershire
Printed and bound in Great Britain by
T. J. International Ltd., Padstow, Cornwall

This book is printed on acid-free paper

For Doris Riley,
Myra Ferguson,
and Patricia Bush

1

It was good to be back in Berkeley, back at her old job in her police sergeant's uniform. As a homicide detective, Marvia Plum worked in plain clothes most of the time, but the option was hers to wear uniform or civvies. And at least for her first few days back on the job, she reveled in the feel of neatly pressed blue wool, the weight of her sidearm on her hip, and the reflection of her brightly polished badge when she passed a glass storefront.

She was doing something she believed in. Society was jaded, and the public viewed police officers as either incompetent bunglers or deadly enemies; many cops had become burnouts, cynics, or worse. Still, Marvia Plum felt that she was doing a useful job. And she was skilled at her work.

Maybe it was a disastrous marriage, an impulsive resignation from the Berkeley Police Department so she could leave the state and join her new husband in Nevada, or the disillusionment and depression that came when she realized how badly she had blundered. Maybe it was all those things that made her understand what she had given up and made her appreciate her old life all the more when she got it back.

She'd spent the first few days studying regs and manuals and case files, bringing herself back up to speed on conditions in the town where she had lived for so many years. Now she picked up her telephone and answered a 911 switched from the dispatcher upstairs. Somebody was dead.

People died every day in a town the size of Berkeley, but mostly of heart attacks or cancer or automobile crashes. Occasionally someone picked a basket full of beautiful wild mushrooms and cooked them for dinner and died of liver failure. Once in a great while an industrial worker got caught in the jaws of a deadly machine and wound up crushed or torn to bits. But this somebody had died in the seemingly safe surroundings of a radio studio, had apparently dropped dead in

2

front of an open mike and an audience of thousands of listeners. When the cry came in to the emergency dispatcher, the caller was hysterical.

The station had received a threat on their community news fax line. The mid-afternoon political show was about to go on the air. If KRED's regular commentator went on the air today, he would die, the message warned. It was worded in a weird broken English. Nobody had taken the threat very seriously. KRED had a reputation for championing unpopular causes; a history of controversy and turmoil. If every threat that came to the station were for real, KRED would have disappeared from the airwaves long ago.

The commentator laughed off the threat. He'd heard it all before. He settled himself in front of the microphone . . . and there he died.

Marvia arrived at KRED three minutes after the message hit her desk. The first people dispatched had been paramedics furnished by the Berkeley Fire Department. Their ambulance stood in front of the KRED building, its roof lights flashing. The station's building was on Berkeley's recently renamed Barbara Jordan Boulevard, just a few blocks from the Hall of Justice on McKinley Avenue. Police headquarters and the city jail were crammed into one outdated building.

As she jumped from the cruiser, Marvia took in the surroundings of the station's two-story terracotta structure. To the left was the Bara Miyako Japanese restaurant. To the right were a couple of retail shops, Bix's Wax Cylinder and the Amazon Rain Forest. A second black-and-white and then a third screeched to the curb beside Marvia's cruiser, and uniformed officers piled out. Marvia signaled to them and they scurried to secure the front and rear entrances of the radio station's building.

Marvia glanced up at the building's theater-like marquee as she hurried through the glass doors: Oceana Network — KRED/FM — One World Radio. Inside, a terrazzo hallway ran between bulletin boards plastered with handbills and posters for public events. The receptionist's post, shielded by a sliding Plexiglas panel, was unoccupied. A second set of glass doors opened into a surprisingly bright lobby. The lobby rose into an atrium; the sliding frosted-glass roof had been rolled back to admit the clear April afternoon's strong sunlight and refreshing air.

Half a dozen people were milling around. Just off the lobby, a door had been smashed, and jagged shards of glass and splinters of polished wood lay on the terrazzo floor. A white-suited EMT turned and spotted Marvia. She asked the young man what he had.

'Fresh cadaver, Sergeant. Still warm, no rigor. Really looks odd — I've never seen such a red complexion.'

'Red as in Navajo?'

'No, I mean red as in tomato, red as in danger flag.'

'What happened to the door?'

'It was locked from the inside. They saw him through the big window. There's a control room.' He pointed. 'There's a big glass window onto the studio where he was. The engineer looked into the studio and saw . . . well. When we got here, nobody could unlock the studio door, so we knocked it down — just in case he was still alive, see. But he wasn't.'

Marvia said, 'Okay,' and stepped past the tech. The man lying across the table in front of a battery of microphones looked plenty dead, and his skin was indeed oddly red. She turned back. 'Do you have any more work to do here?'

'Just some paperwork. The scene is yours now, Sergeant.'

Marvia grunted. If Dispatch was on the ball, the evidence wagon should be arriving in a few minutes. The coroner's people would follow later on. They didn't react with the same urgency as the EMTs or Homicide. Summoning a uniform, Marvia had him secure the studio, including the cadaver and all its other contents, and the smashed door. Then she snagged the nearest civilian, a very young, heavyset woman with pale skin and intense crimson lipstick, wearing a yellow beret.

At Marvia's question the woman identified herself. 'Jessie Loman. I'm a producer. Well, I'm working as receptionist today, but I'm going to be a producer.'

Marvia asked who was in charge. Jessie Loman pointed to a cluster of people swirling around a tall African woman in dreadlocks. 'She's in charge of everything,' the heavyset woman managed. 'Sun Mbolo. She's the station manager.'

Marvia pulled elbows aside and confronted the taller woman. She had always thought of herself as dark-skinned, but she had never seen a person as black as Sun Mbolo. But Ms. Mbolo's skin had the whitish, pasty look that meant she was close to going into shock.

Marvia identified herself. That one word spoken aloud, *police*, could change the atmosphere in a room in a fraction of a second. She hustled Ms. Mbolo to a nearby chair, then turned and ordered the nearest individual to bring a glass of water. Squatting in front of Sun Mbolo's chair, Marvia her hand on the station manager's wrist, in part to offer support and in part to check her pulse and the feel of her skin. The pulse was strong, and the skin didn't have the moist, clammy

7

feeling that Marvia had feared. Sun Mbolo was past the worst moments of her reaction.

'Ms. Mbolo, are you able to help me now? Did you know the dead man?'

'He's Bob Bjorner. He's our chief political analyst. He's dead?' Mbolo asked. 'You're sure he's dead?'

'EMTs are sure of that. The coroner is on the way. This must be quite a blow to you, to lose a friend and colleague this way.' Marvia looked up into the taller woman's thin, finely sculptured features. She must have Ethiopian genes to have that kind of face and those long, slim bones.

Mbolo was shocked but she did not look grief-stricken. 'He was not a friend of mine, and he was not going to be a colleague for long. We were struggling to get rid of Bjorner, and he would not go quietly. We were having a hell of a fight. I am sorry that he is dead, but I will not deny that I am relieved, also. But what a way to go. Right in the studio. About to go on the air. He must have had a heart attack.'

'I doubt that,' Marvia said. 'His skin is bright red. I never heard of a heart attack causing that.'

'Well, a stroke then. Whatever it was, we shall make the proper gesture — perhaps put on a memorial service for him, perhaps broadcast it live. He was with the station for many years, and had a following of old leftists he could rally to his defense when we tried to get him off the air. Let them rally to his defense now.'

Someone approached Marvia. 'Sergeant.' It was one of the police department's evidence techs. The van had arrived and they were ready to go to work.

Marvia addressed the tech. 'Felsner, you people all have booties and gloves, yes?'

'Masks too. Sometimes there's funny stuff in the air. That's a sealed room. We don't know what might come from the cadaver.'

To a uniform Marvia said, 'Look, we can't have all these people milling around. I want the building cleared except — Ms. Mbolo, I want your cooperation — anybody who was in that studio this afternoon or had any contact with the victim. Anybody else, let's get names and contact info and send them home. What about your broadcasting — did KRED go off the air when Bjorner fell over?'

'We switched to live news.'

Marvia inhaled suddenly. 'Oh, no.'

'Yes.' Mbolo was regaining her composure. She actually smiled. 'We have our contingency plan. When something breaks we go to all-news. The earthquake in '89, the fire in '91, Desert Storm . . . we drop everything and just do news.'

'For how long?'

'We will probably cut back to regular programming at four o'clock. We take a satellite feed from Oceana and run it in real time so we can get back to normal quite easily. Then our local news at five. The news department has its own studio and control upstairs. And we can do the evening shows from A.'

'What's that?'

'Mr. Bjorner was broadcasting from Studio B when he passed out. Studio A is a mirror image at the far end of the control booth. We will just do everything from A until we are cleared to get back into B.' She craned her long neck and shook her head at the smashed door. 'We'll have to get that fixed. Those medics, whoever they were, they broke it down. Who's going to pay for it?'

'Those were the emergency medical technicians, Ms. Mbolo. I was told nobody had a key. Isn't that odd?'

'Bjorner was somewhat paranoid. He always locked the studio from the inside. He had a little locking device. You could only open it from his side. He used to lock himself in, then unlock the device when he was ready to leave.'

Marvia said, 'You can file a claim with the city, Ms. Mbolo. Can you run the station without that room for a while?'

'We can do everything from A until we get back B. Everything that is not from Oceana or from news.'

Marvia turned away and surveyed the lobby. The crowd had thinned. How many people did it take to run a radio station, anyway? She'd never been inside one before. She crooked a finger at another uniform. 'Rosetti, I want a quick canvass of the establishments in this block. Talk to the people at that restaurant and the record store and the whatever the heck it is, the fern place. Divide the job with Officer Ng if you need help. Move.'

Rosetti disappeared and Marvia returned her attention to Sun Mbolo. 'Is there someplace where people can go, Ms. Mbolo? The ones who might have some information for us?'

Sun Mbolo nodded. 'There is a conference room. Directly at the head of the stairs.'

'Okay. Listen, you're being very helpful. See if you can herd your people up there. We'll want to talk to them soon and then they can leave, too.'

'What of the news staff?'

'Right. You said you were going to switch to a network program at four?'

'Oceana. We are part of the Oceana One World Network. We take network shows from four to six, then back here for the news and our own evening shows.'

'Okay. Send in the news people at four.

We'll try and get them out first, so they can do their work.' She studied Mbolo's face. 'You don't need to lie down or anything?'

Mbolo pushed herself upright and stood at her full height. She wore an African robe and headcloth. 'I am all right, thank you. I will carry out your instructions, Sergeant.'

Back at Studio B, the evidence technicians were dodging around each other, snapping photos, drawing diagrams, cataloging every item of furniture, every piece of paper and kipple in the room. The fingerprint crew would follow, and the vacuums would pick up every hair, fragment, and loose fiber. A tech would inventory the dead man's pockets and collect his wallet, keys, whatever.

A uniformed officer named Holloway was keeping a harried-looking man in T-shirt and jeans out of the studio. Marvia took charge. 'Who are you?'

'I'm Jem Waller, chief engineer around here. I have to get in there and see what's what. We're running a radio station here, you know?'

Marvia looked into the man's face. 'We're running a potential crime scene here. There's a dead man still in that room. You'll get in when we finish, Mr. Waller.'

The engineer's eyes popped. He nodded angrily and strode away.

Even as the technicians went about their work, Marvia studied the victim and the room. The coroner would make his determination, but Marvia Plum had seen homicides in her life, and she'd seen natural deaths. And she didn't believe there was anything natural about Bjorner's death.

The glasses the fat man had been wearing at the time of death piqued Marvia's curiosity. She'd spotted them the time she'd peered through the doorway, over the shattered door. Now she could get a closer look. The lenses were extremely thick, and one was cracked. The frames looked like something out of an old file photo. Bjorner wore a white dress shirt and a hand-painted tie that had somehow flopped out from under his body. Like the glasses, it was decades out of style. He wore a pair of brown suit pants, badly frayed and dirty, and a pair of scuffed wing-tips. His white hair did not look as clean now as it had from a distance, but his complexion was still a marked, angry red. Marvia looked more closely at his features. It was hard to be sure, especially with the lurid discoloration of his skin, but she thought he might be African American. With a light complexion to start with, and with the peculiar flush, he might look just this way.

The corners of several sheets of paper protruded from beneath his torso. Making a mental note to be sure the pages were collected as evidence, Marvia looked at them more carefully. She'd expected to see a typewritten script, or at least a set of handwritten notes. The white paper was marked with a pattern of raised dots. Was Bjorner's eyesight so bad that he used a Braille script?

But the Braille started one-third of the way down each sheet. At the top of each page, written in what looked like dark crayon, was a day and number: *MON 1,*

MON 2, MON 3. Even a person with very poor eyesight would probably be able to assemble the pages in correct order, then read their contents with his trained fingertips.

A metal wastebasket beside the desk held several empty food containers of the folded cardboard sort with thin wire handles. One container held a spork, one of those ugly plastic spoon-and-fork mutants, and a crumpled paper napkin. There was an ashtray near Bob Bjorner's elbow, and in it several matches, a partially empty matchbook, and the roach of what appeared to be a marijuana cigarette. The matchbook had a logo on the cover and peculiar psychedelic lettering in the shape of swirling naked bodies. It said 'Club San Remo'.

That was intriguing. Marvia had been in the Club San Remo and knew something of its history; she wouldn't expect Bob Bjorner to frequent it. Then she turned away and bent over the shattered door, finding the portable lock that Sun Mbolo had told her Bjorner always used. She signaled an evidence tech and warned her to make sure that the lock was collected. Then she walked thoughtfully back to the station's lobby.

For a moment she was the only person there. She thought about Bob Bjorner, the dead man with the red face and the old-fashioned apparel. He'd been an extremely fat man. It might be possible, after all, that he had died of natural causes — congestive heart failure, something like that.

But the red face haunted her. *Red as in tomato, red as in danger flag.*

2

The yellow crime-scene tape would stay up outside Studio B even though evidence technicians had completed their tasks and the coroner had removed the late Robert Bjorner. The food containers and the marijuana roach would be tested, possibly at the same time Edgar Bisonte, the Alameda county coroner, ran his autopsy on Bjorner. In fact, there was no official crime scene — not yet. That would depend on the determination made by the Alameda county coroner, Edgar Bisonte, M.D. But Marvia was convinced that Bjorner had been poisoned.

She entered the conference room where KRED staff were assembled. A couple of uniforms followed in her wake, and she instructed them to get the statements of everyone in the room. She felt her heart racing with the thrill of the hunt and the excitement of her job.

She loved being a cop. She'd given it up just months before, running off like a hormone-crazed schoolgirl to marry Willie Fergus. Willie had been her mentor years before when she was a military police corporal, halfway around the world and totally at a loss as to what life was about. She and her friends had set out to bed the biggest prizes they could, and Marvia had won the contest, bagging handsome young Lieutenant James Wilkerson. Bagged him, against all regulations bedded him, and then discovered she was pregnant. When Lieutenant Wilkerson heard the news, he'd frozen. This could be the end of his army career. His family had money. If Marvia would have a quiet abortion and say nothing about the matter, she would be taken care of.

She'd appealed to Sergeant First Class Fergus, a man twenty years her senior. He'd guided her through the army's peculiar bureaucratic maze and helped her stand up to the considerable pressure that Lieutenant Wilkerson brought to bear against Corporal Plum. She'd had her baby, and he had his daddy's name on

19

his birth certificate. Lieutenant Wilkerson had been married to the baby's mama when that baby was born, even if he and Marvia had been divorced as soon after that as his lawyers could move the paperwork.

And then, a dozen years later, Marvia had run into Willie Fergus again. By now, Fergus was retired from the army and a sergeant with the Washoe County, Nevada Sheriff's Department. Marvia had been deeply involved with a sweet man named Hobart Lindsey, but the relationship was floundering — as much Marvia's fault as Lindsey's — and here was Willie Fergus to the rescue, all over again. In a trance, Marvia had married him, resigned from the Berkeley Police Department, and moved to Reno. But when she had emerged from her bridal daze, she realized that she had made a dreadful mistake.

Sun Mbolo sat at the head of a polished conference table. Marvia caught her eye and signaled to her. Mbolo rose and glided across the room. Marvia asked her if she had an office where they could talk. Mbolo nodded, and they walked down a carpeted corridor; then she ushered Marvia into the room. She walked around her desk and slid into an executive chair. Marvia closed the office door and seated herself in a chair facing the desk. She opened a snap on her equipment belt. Sometimes she felt like Batgirl, she carried so much paraphernalia, but things came in handy. Then she set a micro-recorder on the desk between them.

'All right if I record our conversation?'

Mbolo said, 'Of course.'

'You say you had a warning that Mr. Bjorner would be killed if he went on the air?'

'That he would die.'

'Do you have the warning?'

'I have the fax.' Mbolo reached for a piece of paper on her desk. Marvia gestured her not to touch it. 'I have already handled it, Sergeant.' Yes, a smart one.

'Just the same.' Marvia picked up the fax with latex-gloved hands. She spread it on the desk in front of her. The fax was date-and-time stamped by the machine. It had come in at 14:58 in the afternoon. Time enough for someone to run to Studio B and warn Bob Bjorner. It was scrawled in childish letters and said: 'three hours murderer stay quite no speke brethe speke no brethe.' There was no signature.

Marvia looked at Mbolo. 'Three hours means three o'clock, do you think?'

'One would so infer.'

'And the rest? 'Stay quite no speke brethe speke no brethe.' What did you think that means?'

'Am I asked to interpret?'

'Ms. Mbolo, I'm asking for your cooperation. A man is dead, and the circumstances are highly suspicious. Your people told us a death threat had been received, and I assume this is it. But I'm not supposed to assume anything, so I ask you again — is this the threat; and if it is, what do you think it means?'

'Aside from the poor spelling and lack of punctuation, I think it means, 'Stay quiet. Do not speak and you will breathe. Speak and you will not breathe.' That is what I think it means, Sergeant.'

Marvia studied the white sheet and its scrawled message. 'This fax doesn't have a source code on it. Do you have any idea where it could have been sent from?'

'None. It could even have come from within the building. There are several fax machines — in the mail room, in the newsroom, in the business office.'

Marvia made a note to have the techs check all the wastebaskets in the building, especially the ones near fax machines, just in case the sender had crumpled up his original when he finished transmitting it and tossed it in the nearest receptacle. A very long shot. Certainly the fax itself was worth keeping. It might be possible to get a handwriting match, although that seemed unlikely, too. The scrawl had the looping, uncontrolled look of a right-handed person writing left-handed to disguise his or her usual penmanship. Or vice-versa. The odd usage and spelling suggested a person with little or no education, or one who was seriously challenged or didn't have much English. Or someone trying to simulate one of those categories. A damned mess! But the case was barely underway. There was a body, there were physical clues, there were plenty of possible perps. Not so bad for starters.

'You told me downstairs that you were not a friend of Mr. Bjorner's, and that you weren't sorry to see him dead. Would you like to elaborate on your statement?'

'Am I being interrogated? Don't you have to read me my rights?'

'Do you want me to?'

Long pause. Finally Mbolo said, 'I was interrogated by the Dirgue. I am not afraid of questioning, believe me.'

Marvia waited.

'The Dirgue were the communist secret police in my country, Ethiopia. Mengistu's people. When you have been questioned by them, nothing else is frightening.' Mbolo smiled thinly.

'Ms. Mbolo, I'm not trying to frighten you. And I'll read you your rights if you want me to. At this point you are not a suspect and I don't think you need your rights. I just want to find out how Robert Bjorner died, and why, and who was responsible for his death. And since you told me you weren't sorry he was dead, I think you'll be able to tell me some other things that might be helpful.'

Sun Mbolo closed her eyes for a moment, then opened them again. 'How much do you know about KRED, Sergeant Plum?'

'Not much. I'll confess, it isn't my favorite station. You used to have a nice jazz show on Sundays, but that seems to be gone now.'

'You do not know the history of this radio station?'

'Not the foggiest.'

'I could give you a brochure.' When Marvia nodded, Mbolo swung around in her chair and reached up to a shelf, then extracted a pamphlet which she held across the desk to Marvia. 'In brief, the station was founded in 1947 by four Berkeley liberal intellectuals. They actually went on the air the following year. A couple of professors from the University of California; both were war veterans. World War Two was only over a couple of years. Another was a fledgling playwright.

The fourth was a woman, a feminist activist.' Mbolo smiled faintly. 'She was far ahead of her time.'

Marvia let her continue.

'The founders did not like what was happening to radio. There was no television on the air — that was yet to come. But they felt there was too much commercialism, the music was vulgar, and the educational potential of the great electronic medium was being wasted on greedy exploitation and — their term — fascistic authoritarianism.'

She paused. Marvia turned the brochure over in her gloved hands. 'Very Berkeley. Who were these founders?'

'There are pictures in the brochure, but I can tell you their names; I have them committed to memory: Peter D'Allessandro, Ruth Rosemere, Isaac Eisenberg, and Jared Kingston. They used their last initials and petitioned the FCC for one of the first FM broadcast licenses on the Pacific Coast.'

Marvia found the page with photos of the four founders. Reorder them and you got Kingston, Rosemere, Eisenberg,

D'Allessandro. KRED.

'But they did not want to glorify themselves,' Mbolo resumed. 'The official motto of the station was 'keep radio educational and democratic'. In fact, that is still our credo.'

Marvia looked up. 'I thought it was Kay-Red. As in left-wing.'

'It was that as well.'

Mbolo was interrupted by a knock at the door. Marvia swung around in her chair. Officer Gutierrez had his knuckle to the glass pane. She signaled him to enter.

'We've got everybody's statement, Sergeant, and the IDs are all kosher. They're kind of restless. They want to get out of that room.'

'Okay, let 'em go.'

Gutierrez pulled the door shut behind him.

'You were saying, Ms. Mbolo — '

'No, you were saying you thought Kay-Red was a left-wing appellation. It was that too. I was not born at the time. Neither were you, I would think. But the old-timers — they say that when the cold

27

war broke out, the founders were shocked. They believed in the worldwide struggle against fascism and imperialism, the United Nations, and so forth. They were appalled by the Berlin airlift, and outraged by the Korean War.'

Marvia wondered what to do with this. It was all history. It could hardly have any connection with the Bjorner murder — or could it? Sometimes if you let them talk they came around to the point and told you wonderful things. She decided to let Mbolo continue.

'For the next forty years, KRED opposed the cold war. It supported the Guzman regime in Guatemala and Fair Play for Cuba Committee, and denounced the Bay of Pigs invasion, the Vietnam War, and US intervention in Nicaragua.'

'But nothing about the Hungarian Revolution, Prague Spring, Poland?' Marvia's years in Germany flashed past. She hadn't been a political soldier. She'd joined the military police, won corporal's stripes, got pregnant, got married, got her discharge, had her baby and divorced her husband. In that order. But she'd seen the

Berlin Wall, and she knew something about conditions in Europe toward the end of the cold war.

'They clucked their tongues,' Mbolo said, 'and regretted the necessity. But it was Western aggression that forced Stalin and Khrushchev and Brezhnev to do the things they did.'

'And you were questioned by the Dirgue in Ethiopia?' Marvia prompted.

'My people were Falasha. *Beta Esrael.*'

'Jews?'

'Most of us are in Israel now, but my family — the Dirgue didn't like us. We were coffee merchants in Gonder. The local party boss decided we were rich Jews hiding gold in our house. We were arrested, my whole family. I was the only one who survived. I walked all the way from Gonder to Djibouti and was able to get political asylum and come to America. I studied at the university, and — it is strange, is it not? Here I am.'

'What about KRED?'

'I took the job because I love radio. I used to listen to it all the time in Gonder. I volunteered here, then I was hired, and now I am station manager. I had to hide how much I hated the communists, is that not strange? But the cold war is over now, and I am trying to return KRED to its roots. Three of the founders are dead. The last survivor — we like to have him back for a special observance once a year, but he is nearly ninety now, and probably will be unable to handle it much longer. But if they were alive, I would want them to be proud of KRED.'

'And that's why you didn't like Bob Bjorner.'

For the first time, Sun Mbolo's face showed anger. 'He was the ultimate apologist for the most vicious of crimes. For everything. For Stalin, for Ceausescu, even Pol Pot and the Khmer Rouge. Yes, and Mengistu. He tried to justify the Dirgue. He knew I was from Ethiopia, but he did not know I am *Beta Esrael*.'

Marvia said, 'Do you have any idea who would want to kill him?'

Mbolo shook her head. 'There was disagreement here in the station between those who wanted to keep the old political line and carry on fighting the cold war in the name of fraternal socialist solidarity, and those who wanted to return to the founders' ideal, 'keep radio educational and democratic'. Those others have no concept of democracy. They think democracy means agreeing with them. Bjorner was one of the worst. Sincere enough, I think, in his own way — but totally convinced that he was objectively and incontrovertibly correct. Ergo, anyone who disagreed with him was wrong. He made many people very angry with him here at KRED, but I do not think any of them would kill him.'

'*Someone* killed him, Ms. Mbolo.'

'You are sure of that?'

Marvia ignored the question. 'Where were you when he died?'

'When did he die?'

After some more fencing, Mbolo was able to account for her afternoon. Marvia would have to collect the statements the uniforms had got from everyone else in the station from the time of Bjorner's arrival to the time of his death, and do a mix-and-match with them. She'd want a report from Edgar Bisonte's office in

Oakland, and the sooner the better. And she'd want to check out Bjorner's home and family situation.

'One more thing, Ms. Mbolo . . . How did you get the job of station manager? You said you'd been a volunteer here, but had you ever worked elsewhere, in radio?'

Mbolo was silent.

'Is that a sore point?' Marvia asked.

'This was my first broadcast experience. In fact, for the promotion I was jumped over several people who had been here longer than I. Much longer. Naturally, there was a certain amount of resentment.'

Naturally. 'How did that happen?'

Mbolo steepled her long fingers. 'The previous manager was under a certain amount of pressure. You know, there was a difficult permit process involved in having this building constructed. The old Oceana/KRED offices up on Spalding Street — do you know them?'

'I remember passing by.'

'KRED was in there from the very beginning. The place was poor at best, and as the years passed, it became an utter eyesore. I mean, our programmers would arrange for the presence of guests, world-famous authors and musicians as well as scientists and educators, and it was an embarrassment. So KRED and Oceana raised a capital fund. The usual pleas over the air, surely you have heard them — 'Send us a hundred dollars, send us five dollars, send us anything you can, we need your help.''

'I've heard them many times.'

'Meanwhile, we had fund-raisers in the field running guilt scenarios on corporate donors and foundations and a few very liberal philanthropists. And of course our dear friends, as we call them, the Feds. We get a lot of money from the government.'

'But you blast the government every day. At least, that's KRED's reputation.'

Mbolo smiled and spread her hands.

'All right,' Marvia resumed. 'Let's get back to the point. How you got this job.'

'There were some permit problems and a major tax abatement issue, and we had to appeal to our friends on the city council — especially our champion there, council member Hanson. I will say our manager did a grand job — the way was smoothed before us; but then there were nasty questions raised about the permits and the taxes and the overly familiar relationship between KRED and Ms. Hanson's office. Ultimately, the board at Oceana felt that our station manager was garnering too much unfavorable publicity.' She placed her elbows on her desk and leaned toward Marvia. 'So she moved up to a less visible job with Oceana, and someone with a much lower, much less controversial profile at KRED was elevated to the Awful Office. And here I am.'

'You say your predecessor moved up to Oceana? This was punishment?'

'Not punishment, Sergeant Plum. Protection.'

Marvia nodded. She'd seen that kind of move before, both in the army and in the police department. It was all too common a maneuver. 'What was this person's name? And where is she now?'

'Her name is Parlie Sloat, Sergeant, and she is still at Oceana. Right in this very building.'

Marvia made a mental note to chat with Parlie Sloat at some point. There seemed no particular connection between her and Robert Bjorner, but at this early stage in the case, a great deal remained to be learned. In the meanwhile, there were more immediate matters to pursue.

She sent a uniform to fetch Jessie Loman, the receptionist in the vivid lipstick and the bright yellow beret. Then she moved to the conference room, now deserted, and waited until Officer Rosetti, a bright female a decade younger than herself, showed up with Loman.

'I already gave my statement,' Loman complained. 'It's getting late and I have to get home. I'm officially off duty now. I have a date tonight.'

'We'll make it fast.'

'I mean, I'm sorry Mr. Bjorner died, but I have a date.'

'Okay. Sit down and relax. You want to call your boyfriend and tell him you'll be a little late? This shouldn't take very long.'

Loman pouted for a moment, then she said, 'If you promise it really won't take long, I guess it'll be okay.'

Marvia nodded. 'Thank you.' She'd removed the microcassette with her conversation with Sun Mbolo on it, labeled it and slipped it in her pocket. For Jessie Loman she started a new cassette. 'I just want to ask you a few questions, mainly about Mr. Bjorner. Did you know him well, Jessie?'

'Not very.'

'I thought he was an old-timer here at KRED.'

'I guess so. I've only been here a few months. I want to be a producer. I used to listen to *OTR Heaven* and I got interested and came to KRED.'

Marvia nodded. 'What's OTR?'

'Old-time radio. You know, like they had in the thirties and forties. Shows like *The Shadow* and *Inner Sanctum*. Lon Dayton does an OTR show; I wrote him letters about it, and I'm learning to be a producer. But I have to work as receptionist the rest of the time.'

Marvia put that away for future reference. 'Was Bob Bjorner blind?'

'Not exactly. He could see a little. And

he didn't want anybody to help him. I remember when I started working at KRED, the first day when Bob came in to do his show, he looked as if he knew his way around and he could see everything. He had on these Coke-bottle glasses and his eyes looked weird, but that was just distortion.' She paused and looked at her wristwatch. It had the KRED logo on its face, a little red radio with the station's call letters spelled out in jagged lightning bolts. She cleared her throat. 'And then, there was a package on the floor. UPS had just delivered a shipment of CDs for the music department. Somebody was supposed to put it away, but it was still in the hallway and Bob tripped over it and fell down. He was a heavy man, you know.'

Marvia nodded.

'He had a hard time getting up,' Loman continued. 'I came out from behind the switchboard and tried to help him, and he got bright red and started screaming at me. He was really mad. I don't think he hurt himself falling, but I think he felt humiliated. Then he went into Studio B

and did his show like nothing happened.'
Jessie Loman shook her head. 'He didn't
like people to see his scripts, either. He
used Braille scripts. So I guess his eyes
were really bad, I mean really, or he
wouldn't have needed to use Braille
scripts, would he?'

'No, he wouldn't,' Marvia agreed. 'Do
you know how he lost his vision? Did he
always have bad eyes?'

'I remember they did an anniversary
show, the end of World War One. Or Two.
Whichever. Nikki put together this
documentary; she interviewed Mr. Bjorner. I never heard him open up like that,
just only that once. He said he got burned
by white phosphorus on Tarawa. That's
an island.'

'Yes.'

'I don't think he had any scars or
anything, but I guess that's what hurt his
eyes.'

Marvia changed tack. 'How did he get
to KRED to do his show?'

'His brother always brings him and
drops him off and picks him up
afterward. I don't know what he does

while Bob's here. I mean, while he was here. He didn't come inside the station. I just saw him once in a while when he dropped Bob off or picked him up. Some of the staffers hang out around the corner at Shaughnessy's, on Huntington, but I don't know if Mr. Bjorner — the other Mr. Bjorner — ever did that. Bob used to go next door for a snack after his show, or sometimes to Shaughnessy's for a glass of wine. But he always came back here and waited for his ride.'

'What's this brother's name?'

'Herb. Herb Bjorner.'

'Do you have an address for either brother?'

Loman shook her head. 'No. Bob was kind of paranoid. He didn't like people to know where he lived. He always picked up his paycheck and his mail at the station.'

'Okay.'

'As a matter of fact, I can give you a directory of station personnel. It has addresses and phone numbers, but of course we only have what people give us.'

'Please, yes.'

'I'll have to go get it.'

'I'll go with you.'

The list was longer than Marvia had expected. Loman explained that KRED used a lot of volunteers and part-time people. Marvia folded the list and slipped it into a pocket. She looked at her own wristwatch. 'Thanks for your cooperation, Ms. Loman. You'll probably be asked to help us out later on. We appreciate your assistance.'

Jessie Loman got up and headed for the stairs. Marvia followed her. The crime scene was cleared now. The glass shards outside Studio B had been swept up, the smashed door was removed, and KRED seemed to have returned to normal. Robert Bjorner was on his way to the county morgue, in downtown Oakland, subject to the tender ministrations of the coroner. The evening news was on; concealed speakers carried the station's programming into the lobby atrium. A smooth voice was describing a shouting match in the Oakland city council over who would pick up the bills for a hundred million dollars' worth of defaulted stadium construction bonds.

Last to leave. Marvia found herself longing for her old apartment on Oxford Street, a turret room in a gorgeous Victorian that had long since been split into rental units. That was gone forever, but she had to get another place of her own. She was going stir crazy back on Bonita Street. Or maybe, she thought, she was just tired and hungry. The thrill of being back at work had passed.

She heaved a sigh and pushed open the frosted-glass doors, then stepped onto the sidewalk and bounced off something huge and soft and warm.

It was a man's belly.

3

She staggered back and bounced off the door. Her right hand moved to her holster and her fingers reached for the snap that secured her S&W .40 automatic. Night had fallen, but light from a streetlamp combined with the glow that penetrated the frosted glass of the KRED doors was sufficient to show her the man she had collided with. He looked a lot like Bob Bjorner, but a little thinner and younger. And his skin wasn't bright red. It was the khaki-tan shade, suggesting mixed ancestry. His hair was crinkly, his eyes a pale blue.

An old woman swathed in sagging layers of colorless sweaters stopped and watched the encounter. She was singing something unrecognizable and nodding vigorously to an invisible companion. 'Move along, please,' Marvia urged the old woman.

The woman waved her arms like a bird

trying to take wing. 'You need help, sister? Is this bruiser bothering you?'

Marvia moved toward the woman. 'There's nothing happening here, ma'am. Please just move along.'

The woman spun around and wandered back toward Huntington Way. That was all Marvia needed now, a street crazy on her hands. She focused on the big man. 'Are you Herbert Bjorner?'

The man nodded. Behind him, a huge Oldsmobile ticked like a time bomb. Probably just the engine cooling. It was parked behind Marvia's cruiser. Bjorner tried to push past Marvia, but she stopped him with a hand on his wrist. He said, 'Let me in. My brother — let me past, please.'

Marvia stepped back. Bjorner tried the frosted-glass doors but they wouldn't open. They'd locked automatically behind Marvia. Bjorner cursed.

Marvia said, 'There's nothing to see in there. Did you know — '

'Bobby's dead,' Bjorner said.

'That's right. I'm sorry. Were you notified, Mr. Bjorner?'

'I heard it on KRED. I dropped Bobby off like always and went home and lay down. I haven't been feeling too good lately; I was a little worried about my health. And what would happen to Bobby if anything happened to me.'

'And you had your radio tuned to KRED?'

'Bobby has one of the old monitors, sure. But I must have dozed off. I woke up and heard Nikki Klein's voice doing the KRED news. She was talking about Bobby's years of faithful service to the cause. A fighter who would be missed.'

'You knew then?'

'No.' Bjorner shook his head. 'I thought she was talking about him going off the air. I know they've been trying to dump the old-timers. Sun Mbolo, Serita Sunset, Willem O'Hare, Sojourner Strength, Lon Dayton, that whole disgusting bunch. They were trying to get rid of all the real movement people, the fighters, the strong revolutionary fronters. I thought there had been a coup at KRED and they were finally firing everybody who wouldn't turn their coats and join the capitalist

sellout gang that's running KRED now.'
He paused, looking flushed.

'Are you all right? Do you need any medication?'

He waved his hand dismissively. 'You know what they were doing to Bob? Salami tactics. Your opponent starts with the salami and you start with the knife, and you take a tiny slice off the end, and another tiny slice, so thin he hardly notices each one, but you keep slicing and taking and eventually you have the whole salami.'

'What's the point?'

'Bob used to have a two-hour time slot. He was the heart and soul of KRED. They cut him to an hour, then to a half-hour three times a week, then this latest round they stripped him.'

Marvia frowned. 'Stripped?'

'They put him on Monday through Friday, three o'clock every afternoon.'

'What's wrong with that?'

'Fifteen minutes a day. What kind of serious theme can you develop in fifteen minutes? But Bob took it; he swallowed his pride and started running multi-part

45

programs. They didn't like that either, that Mbolo creature and the rest of her gang, the KRED Hebrew Lesbian Alliance. They wanted him to go on live on the morning show, three five-minute mini-segments a day, five days a week. You understand the tactic? You can't fire the man — even Mbolo didn't have that kind of balls — so you make his life so tough he can't keep up, and he either quits or you have an excuse to dump him off the air.' He grinned bitterly. 'Then they can start taking oil money like PBS, the Petroleum Broadcasting System. Bob would have stopped 'em. He would have been the last holdout at the barricades; he would have blown the roof off. So they got rid of him this way instead. Now they're rid of everybody. Radio Red was their biggest enemy. Mbolo's probably with her pals right now, celebrating. She'll dance on Bobby's grave, the bitch.'

'Okay,' Marvia said, 'then when did you learn of your brother's death?'

'She kept on going. She's on the side of the people. Not as committed as she should be, but she's trying. Then she wrapped up by repeating the headlines, and one of them was that Bobby was dead. Right there in the studio. So I came back. It took me a while, but I came back.'

Marvia said, 'Mr. Bjorner, I think you should go home. You can't get into the station now, and there's nothing there to see. Your brother's remains have been taken by the county coroner. You may have to go down to Oakland and identify him in the morning. And we'll need to ask you some questions.'

'He was murdered,' Bjorner said. 'He knew they were going to get him. You know he always brought his special lock to the studio?'

'I know about that, yes.'

'He expected a mail bomb. He knew it was a right-wing conspiracy. He thought they'd get him in the studio. Remember that gunman at KGO a few years ago? Bobby was expecting something like that.' He looked into Marvia's face. 'How did they get him?'

'Mr. Bjorner, we don't know that your

brother was murdered at all. He might have died of natural causes.' But she didn't believe that. Not with the scarlet face she had seen. In death, Radio Red had lived up to his name.

'He was murdered, all right. He was going to blow the roof right off of everything. But they got him before he could get them.'

'Mr. Bjorner,' Marvia said, 'I can give you a ride home. In the police unit. You can come back for your car in the morning. I'll make sure you don't get a ticket.'

Bjorner shook his head. 'No. I'll drive home.'

'I'll need your address, please. And phone number. We'll need to contact you.' Marvia took out her notebook and pen and waited.

Bjorner looked at her for a long time, then said: 'All right. It's unlisted. But I suppose it's all right.' He gave her an address in north Berkeley and shook his head. 'Helping the police. Bobby must be whirling.'

Marvia gave him her card and waited

while he climbed back into the Oldsmobile. The sedan tilted with his weight. Bjorner pulled away from the curb and headed north on Barbara Jordan Boulevard.

4

Marvia Plum turned in her cruiser at Berkeley police headquarters and dragged herself upstairs. She was suddenly bone-weary. The adrenaline rush of the run to KRED and the feeling of getting back to work had lifted her to the heights, and now that the adrenaline rush had ended she crashed like a cocaine addict when the drug wore off.

She locked up her uniform and equipment and luxuriated in a long, hot shower. She scrubbed her close-cropped hair with shampoo and rinsed it. By the time she toweled off, she could feel her skin start to breathe again. She pulled on a pair of jeans and a sweatshirt, then took her personal weapon, a little .38 Airweight revolver, out of her locker and tucked it into her waistband.

She left the Hall of Justice and pulled her tan-and-cream Mustang out of the parking lot, onto McKinley Avenue on the short drive home. At Bonita Street, Marvia pulled the Mustang into the driveway and locked the car. She climbed the wooden steps to the veranda and slipped her key into the front-door lock, then stepped inside the foyer.

The sound of a network talk show was coming from the living room. Her widowed mother was home from work and relaxing. Marvia made her way upstairs, passing her son Jamie's room — once her brother Tyrone's — and heard the squeaks and bleeps of a Nintendo. She paused and heard Jamie's voice and his friend Hakeem White's.

Managing a weary smile, she entered her own bedroom, where she slipped the revolver from her waistband and locked it in a case that she replaced on her closet shelf. She crossed the hall again and knocked on Jamie's door and let herself into his room. Jamie let Hakeem finish the Nintendo game as he bounced across the room and hugged Marvia. 'Can Hakeem stay for dinner?' Marvia smiled and said he could. Then, reluctantly, she went downstairs.

Gloria Plum looked up when Marvia walked into the living room. 'I didn't hear you come in. You could have said hello.'

'You were watching TV. And I just needed a minute to myself. You wouldn't have wanted to see me in the shape I was in.'

Gloria clicked the TV remote. 'You going to cook tonight, Marvia?'

'I was hoping you would. Mom, I caught a homicide today. Probable homicide — I have to hear from Bisonte.'

Gloria looked up at her daughter. 'You're home now, Marvia.'

'I know. Jamie's friend Hakeem is staying for dinner.'

'Nobody asked me,' Gloria said.

Marvia sighed. 'I'll order pizza.'

Gloria pointed the remote at the TV and the screen sprang back to life. Marvia picked up the cordless telephone and dialed a pizza delivery. She knew everyone's preference. After she'd given the order, she went out onto the porch and sat down.

She felt a pang and realized she was missing her father. Marcus's death had been more a release than a loss; it had broken Marvia's heart to see him fading. She was over it now, but once in a while she let her guard down, and then she would feel the catch in her throat and the sting in her eyes.

Maybe that was why she had dumped sweet, timid Hobart Lindsey and married Willie Fergus. When their paths crossed again, he as a sheriff's department sergeant in Reno and she as a cop in Berkeley, she had been quick to accept his offer of marriage. She didn't know that he expected to own her.

A pair of headlights turned onto Bonita, and Marvia hurried down the steps and to the curb before the driver could cruise past.

★　★　★

Gloria and Marvia sat at the head and foot of the dinner table; Jamie and Hakeem faced each other across its width. They talked about their school-work and Nintendo games and about trying out for the Benjamin Banneker

Junior High baseball team. They were a shortstop/second base combination and they were going to play together for Berkeley High and UC, then go to the big leagues as a team.

'So you caught a homicide?' Gloria said.

Marvia gave a start. She'd been listening to the boys make their plans and was a million miles away from the crimson-faced corpse sprawled on the table in front of the microphone. She'd have to call in a consultant to tell her what Radio Red's last script said; what the little Braille dimples meant.

'Marvia?'

'Mom. I've been getting caught up. I was lucky to get my job back. And my stripes.'

'A good thing you did. How did you think you were going to meet your responsibilities, Marvia?'

Marvia clenched her teeth. She wasn't going to get drawn into this argument again. Gloria had never forgiven her for divorcing James Wilkerson, Jamie's dad.

'They had it on the early edition of the

news,' Gloria said as she lifted a slice of pizza and nibbled at its pointed tip. 'They showed the radio station and they had a telephone interview with the manager, that Sunny woman.'

'Sun, Mom. Sun Mbolo. She's from Ethiopia. Anyway, it looks like a homicide, but it might not have been. I mean, the man must have weighed three hundred pounds, and he was old.'

Gloria raised one eyebrow. 'How old?'

'He was seventy-two. We got his birth records, everything. He fought in the Pacific; he was an old man.'

'Someday you won't think seventy-two is so old.'

Marvia looked at the two boys. Each was on his third slice of pizza, and neither of them carried an ounce of fat on his body. She shook her head. 'I think you're right, Mom.'

After dinner, Gloria retired to the living room couch. Marvia made coffee and carried a cup and saucer for herself and one for her mother. Gloria dipped her head toward the table and Marvia set the coffee down. Gloria had turned on the TV but muted the sound so she could concentrate on the telephone.

Jamie and Hakeem were putting away the few dishes that had been used at the meal. Marvia asked if they had homework to do. Jamie dipped his head a millimeter.

'Do you need help?

'No, Mom.'

'No, Ms. Plum.'

'Then you'd better get to it. Hakeem, what time is your mother expecting you home?'

'Ten o'clock.'

'Then you'd better get to work.'

The boys disappeared upstairs, headed for Jamie's room. Marvia took her own cup of coffee upstairs and set it on the night table. She realized that she hadn't eaten a bit of the pizza. She pulled up her sweatshirt and looked at her belly. Maybe could do without pizza. Besides, being a cop didn't mean you had to live on cop food.

She turned on her tuner and found the KRED signal. Somebody was playing a scratchy record of an early Louis Armstrong Hot Seven performance. When the music ended, a peculiar voice, both scratchy and whispery, announced the full personnel on the track. He made no mention of Bob Bjorner's death, but that didn't strike Marvia as strange. It was a long programming day and KRED announcers couldn't talk about Bjorner constantly.

'This is your master wax-miner, Little Bix, bringing the music of the past into the night of the present. Don't you wish you'd been in the studio with Louis and Lil and Baby Dodds and the rest of the folks when they laid that down? Long ago and far away, my friend. Now for a change, we'll hear the queen of the blues, Ma Rainey herself.'

The music started, and the voice began singing 'Toad Frog Blues.' Marvia put her head on her pillow and closed her eyes.

Little Bix.

One of KRED's neighbors was Bix's Wax Cylinder, and the whispery-scratchy man called himself Little Bix. Jessie Loman had talked about how many volunteers and part-timers KRED used. People who had other jobs, other lives to live.

Little Bix might have appropriated the name from Leon Beiderbecke, the original Bix. The store, the station, the whispery-scratchy man. Was he one of Bjorner's faithful, or one of the sellout gang? If there was internecine war at KRED, could it go so far that a disc jockey would murder a political commentator? That seemed absurd, but people had killed people over political disputes before.

Marvia fell asleep, and when she woke up she blinked at the digital clock beside her bed; it was after eleven. A thumping sound was going on, but after a few seconds she was able to identify it as music. She sat up and stood on the carpet. She was still wearing her sweatshirt and jeans, woolen socks and no shoes. When she opened her door, the thumping got louder.

Her first thought was about her mother. Gloria went to bed early on weeknights. She had a responsible job with the Social Security Administration and she commuted every day to Richmond, a dozen miles up the freeway. If

Jamie's music disturbed her sleep, there would be an explosion.

Marvia knew she had to move out of this house and take her son with her. Gloria had been generous about keeping Jamie when Marvia moved to Nevada. He'd lived with her and Marcus while Marvia was single and living on Oxford Street, and he'd stayed on when she remarried. And Gloria had been generous about Marvia moving into Bonita Street when she returned to Berkeley. But there was no domestic tranquillity here, and the sooner Marvia and Jamie got out the better.

Padding silently down the hall to Jamie's room, Marvia tapped at the door and turned the knob. There was a frantic scrambling inside the room. Even before Marvia could get the door open, the volume of the music dropped dramatically and she heard a window being opened. She stepped into the room and with her first breath recognized the familiar odor of cannabis.

Jamie was shoving something under the mattress of his bed and Hakeem was closing a dresser drawer. Marvia shut the door behind her. The two boys faced her. Their faces were identical studies in terror.

Marvia said nothing, waiting for one of them to make the first move. Jamie dropped his gaze. He murmured a few words. Marvia said, 'Speak up, young man. And look me in the eye when you speak to me.'

Jamie raised his eyes and said, 'I guess we're busted.'

Marvia nodded. 'You'd better take that out from under your mattress before you start a fire.'

Jamie bent over and lifted the edge of his mattress. He came back up with a makeshift ashtray, a soup bowl with a roach in a roach clip shaped like three intertwined human figures, and a disposable butane lighter.

Marvia turned to Hakeem. 'Your turn, Mr. White.'

The boy trembled visibly as he pulled open a drawer in Jamie Wilkerson's dresser. Then he turned back toward her and held up a cellophane bag. Under the ceiling light of Jamie's room, Marvia could see the dark-green buds and the neat little package of rolling papers.

'I'm sorry, Ms. Plum. I never did this before. It was my fault. I brought the stuff over. Jamie didn't know anything about it.'

'Jamie, is that true?'

He shook his head. She didn't like the expression on his face but he said, 'No, it isn't. It's my weed. I gave some to Hakeem. No way it's his.'

At least they were both being men. They wouldn't rat out a buddy to save their own necks. 'Don't you boys know better than to do this? All else aside, you put me in a very difficult position. I'm a sworn police officer. I can't just ignore this.'

'So write us a summons,' Jamie said. 'Like a parking ticket. Big deal.'

They were all keeping their voices down, caught in a tacit bond. Nobody wanted to bring Gloria Plum into the room.

'That's for adults, boy. You've got a long, *long* way to go before you're an adult. How would you like a trip to Juvenile Hall?'

The boys remained silent.

'Where did you get the grass?'

Hakeem said, 'Everybody has it at school. You can get it anyplace. Ho Chi Minh Park. Over by the baseball diamond. You know, where Blue Beetle and Acid Alice hang out.'

That was no surprise to Marvia. She said, 'Hakeem, here's your choice. You'll tell your parents about this and they'll phone me to discuss it. Will you do that?'

The boy looked as if he wanted to pull his head in between his shoulders like a turtle.

'Your other choice is, I'll call them. Now, how about it?'

He hesitated, then said, 'Okay. I'll tell — does it matter which one?'

'Either or both. Now you get out of here. I want you to go straight home. If I don't hear from your mom or dad in twenty-four hours, they'll hear from me.'

Hakeem slunk out of the room. Marvia waited until she heard the front door of the house open and close. Then she looked at her son. Her heart was racing and she had trouble catching her breath.

Jamie said, 'At least he has a mom and dad. At least they make a home for Hacker.'

Marvia closed her eyes and put her hand on the wall to steady herself. 'Blue Beetle and Acid Alice. I don't want you anywhere near those thugs. They belong in prison.' They were two of Berkeley's counter-culture icons; they'd been suspected of dealing drugs but never arrested. 'Have you tried those drugs? What drugs have you tried? I want the whole truth from you, right now.'

'Hack and me, we just shared a joint.'

'Nothing else?'

He looked sheepish. 'Couple of brews.'

Marvia let out her breath. 'Don't you have a DARE instructor at your school?'

'Yeah.' He was looking out the window. 'Jennie Steinberg. That's one of those Hymie names, isn't it?'

'It's her name, that's all it is!'

'Sure. She's not a real cop anyhow. She doesn't even have a gun.'

Marvia's chest felt tight. What kind of

mother had to carry a gun to win the respect of her son? She said, 'I know Officer Steinberg. She's a good cop. I worked with her for a year, on patrol. She has what it takes, Jamie, and for your information she's a better shot than I am.'

He'd turned back from the window and was paying attention.

'Don't you believe the things you learn in the DARE classes?'

'The little kids do. The big ones just laugh at that stuff. Hack and me toke up once in a while, so what?'

She hated to fall back on the old lines, but she couldn't fight him any longer. 'I'm your mother, and I have a duty to guide you. God gave you to me, and I'm responsible for you. When you're a man you'll make your own decisions. Until then you will listen to me.'

He grunted.

She said, 'I'll see you in the morning. Six o'clock, Jamie. Set your alarm. I want to see you washed and dressed in clean clothes. At the breakfast table. And you'd better bring a good attitude with you.'

He said, 'Okay.'

She managed to kiss her son good night; his cheek was like granite. 'And, Jamie, do I need to tell you, you're grounded until further notice. Until we get this worked out.'

'But mom! Baseball tryouts are next week. Hack and me are gonna make the Clockers!'

'Grounded. Period. School and home. Period.'

5

Gloria Plum liked her own company better than that of anyone else. For years she had made it a point to rise early, eat breakfast alone and leave the house before other family members came downstairs. Marvia had thought that was cruel in Marcus's last years, but today she was relieved not to have to face both her mother and her son over the breakfast table. Jamie would be more than enough.

Marvia was preparing a breakfast of scrambled eggs and toast with marmalade when Jamie came down. The swinging door seemed to hesitate once, then sweep inward. Jamie wore an Oakland Raiders cap with the bill turned sideways, a T-shirt featuring a larger-than-life portrait of an angry black man, baggy jeans and sneakers. He sat down at the table.

Marvia said, 'Hat off.'

He glared at her but complied.

66

'Have you thought about what happened last night?'

'What happened to my stash?'

'You're lucky, Jamie. I got mad and threw it away. So now I've destroyed evidence and you and Hakeem are in the clear.'

'I told you that Hakeem had nothing to do with it. It was my dope. Could I have my roach clip back? That was expensive. And it's just a roach clip, it's not illegal.'

'It's drug paraphernalia and it is definitely illegal. Have you talked with your friend? Did you call him last night or this morning?'

'No.' He scowled.

Marvia set out their meal. She never had eaten any pizza last night and she realized that she was hungry. 'I expect to hear from Hakeem's parents, Jamie, or I'm going to call them myself. This is serious business.'

'What are you going to do, call my dad? He in Washin'ton playin' up to all ob de white folks, ain' he?'

Marvia barely restrained herself from slapping her son. 'You will not use that

Tomming dialect in this house, or anywhere! Never!'

'My mama the sellout. When are they going to give you a talk show?'

She decided to change her tack. 'Did you finish your homework? Or were you and your friend too stoned last night to do any?'

'It's all done.'

'I want to see it before you go to school.'

'The dog ate it.'

Marvia stood up. Jamie grinned and tucked into his scrambled eggs. Marvia had lost her appetite. 'Finish your breakfast and put your dishes in the washer before you go to school. And I want you to come straight home from your last class and study until your grandma and I get home. I just might phone you any time. In fact you can be sure that I'll call, that's a promise, and you'd better be here when I do.'

She hurried back upstairs, retrieved her .38 Airweight and tucked it into her waistband. Then she clipped a pair of handcuffs onto a belt loop behind her back. She intended to get rolling seriously on the Bjorner case today, and she would be most effective, she decided, in civvies.

As she pulled the Mustang out of the driveway and headed north to McKinley, Marvia decided she needed to talk with somebody about what was going on in her life. For a moment she considered phoning James Wilkerson. He was Jamie's biological father, and he might have some influence with the boy. But Wilkerson had never shown much interest in Jamie. The only time he'd paid attention was not long after Desert Storm, when Jamie was onboard an antique bomber and in danger of losing his life, and James Senior had a chance to be a hero and make headlines. Good press for a would-be congressman, and Wilkerson was now a member in good standing of the United States House of Representatives. No point in calling him, Marvia decided. He wouldn't want the trouble, and if she pushed him too hard he might just make another attempt to get Jamie away from her. She shivered.

Her second husband was worse than

the first, and the man she'd had between them . . . She shook her head and wanted to kick herself. He hadn't been a great physical specimen, he wasn't the world's most sparkling personality, and he was white: one-two-three strikes you're out at the old ball game. But he was the best man she'd ever known, except for her father, and she'd shined him on; now he was living in a glitzy high-rise in Denver and climbing a corporate pyramid. He was out of California and out of her life and —

Brakes screamed. Marvia gasped, hit her own brakes, swung the wheel and missed a FedEx van by a hair. She sat clutching her steering wheel and shaking. She'd gone so deep into her self-pitying reverie that she'd run the red light at Ashby, one of the busiest streets in the city. She was lucky she hadn't been killed, or killed somebody else.

When the light changed again, she crept through the intersection and continued on to work. It wasn't even eight o'clock in the morning and already her day was a depressing pile of compost.

She found a stack of paper on her desk, including a note from Dorothy Yamura: 'Come see me.'

She sank into her chair and leafed through the stack of paper. A few routine memos, and a number of interviews and crime-scene reports from KRED. That was good, anyhow. Nothing from the lab or the coroner's office, though. A call-back slip from Angelina Tesla at the DA's office.

She had to clear her mind of her personal problems. Gloria had always been a difficult mother; but since the death of Marvia's dad, Marcus, she had become impossible. And Jamie smoking dope in his room with Hakeem — Marvia knew that marijuana itself was a mild enough drug, but it put her into an untenable position as a sworn police officer. Besides, if Jamie and Hakeem were starting to move with the drug crowd . . . She didn't even want to think about it, but she had to. Maybe she should talk to Tyrone. He was Jamie's favorite uncle — his only uncle; the only positive adult male figure in the family.

And she did love her brother, and enjoyed his company. She'd ask him to help out.

In the meanwhile, she sent off a memo to Inspector Stillman in Narcotics. She'd gone undercover once on a narco bust, with mixed results. She and her team had failed to prevent a murder, but they'd made a collar that stuck and put away not only the killer but several of his associates, including the club owner, Solomon San Remo. And wasn't that an amusing coincidence: here was Solomon San Remo again, connected with the late Robert Bjorner. Except that Solly was in prison. That Marvia knew for a fact.

She asked Stillman for an informal briefing on Blue Beetle and Acid Alice, then tried to put the matter out of her mind. It was time for work now.

She called Tesla first. She learned nothing useful from the assistant DA, but she hadn't really expected to. It was important to keep that line of communication open. Next, she called the county coroner's office in Oakland and spoke to a coroner's tech named Gemma Silver. Marvia introduced herself and asked

Silver if there was an autopsy yet on Bjorner.

'Sorry, Sergeant. We're just a little behind, as usual. Hold the phone; I'll check the schedule.'

Marvia let her eyes rove the room while she waited. She must have been emanating angry rays. Nobody wanted to make eye contact.

'Two o'clock this afternoon, Sergeant. Dr. Bisonte's going to handle it himself. You want to attend?'

Marvia shook her head. 'Not if I can help it. I know what three hundred pounds of blubber looks like. I just want to know the results ASAP.' But she knew that she *would* attend the autopsy. It was department policy. 'I want to know cause of death. Think I can get that today?'

'Well, I've peeped at the cadaver. Golly, what a whale! I'd guess a massive heart attack. Second choice, stroke.'

'No autopsy yet and you're giving me cause of death, Silver?'

'I'm just giving you an educated guess, Sergeant.'

'Yeah, sure. Listen to me, just in case

Dr. Bisonte isn't feeling too committed to his work today, would you remind him that I'd like a report on the contents of the decedent's stomach?'

'That's SOP, Sergeant.'

'Fine. Just don't overlook it, will you? And don't throw anything away, for God's sake.'

'Got it. Look, I've got another call. Is there anything else?'

Marvia said no and hung up. She called the forensics lab. Laura Kern took the call. That was good. She knew Kern; had worked with her before and had confidence in her. She asked if there was a report on the contents of the ashtray in Studio B, or the food containers in the wastebasket. Nothing yet. That was to be expected. Marvia was just getting impatient, jittery, more because of her home situation than the Bjorner case; but when one spilled over and impacted the other, she knew it would lead to bad police work on her part. She stood up and went to see Lieutenant Dorothy Yamura.

Yamura tilted her head toward a client chair and Marvia settled into it. Yamura was wearing a tan tweed jacket over a pink button-down shirt. A pair of reading glasses shaped liked twin teacups sat on her nose. She looked like a stern librarian. Before Marvia said a word, Yamura asked how well she was settling back into routine.

Marvia hesitated, then replied, 'Just great, Lieutenant.'

Yamura peered at Marvia over the top of her glasses. 'You're a lousy liar, you know that?'

'Well,' Marvia conceded, 'glass half-full, glass half-empty. You know.'

Yamura flipped the pages on her desk calendar. 'You want to talk about it, off duty, after hours, off the reservation?'

'Off the record, too?'

'Woman to woman and friend to friend. I'll buy you dinner. How about — let me check my calendar — how about Saturday night? I'll pick you up at your house.' Marvia nodded. Yamura scribbled on her calendar and dropped her glasses so they hung on her chest by their chain. When she removed the glasses, she shifted gears. 'Guess who called me this morning, demanding action on this death over at KRED?'

Marvia didn't have to guess. 'City council member Hanson.'

'Bull's eye. Now, for double or nothing, what did she have to say?'

'What's wrong with the BPD, can't we protect a vital community asset like KRED, Bob Bjorner was a pillar of the community and of civic thought, and if this was one of those right-wing rant-stations in San Francisco they would have the case wrapped up by now.'

With a thin smile, Yamura said, 'If you had a crystal ball you could set up shop and make a fortune. You know that Hanson is getting restless at city hall. She has her eye on Sacramento. Or maybe, I don't know, Washington. She's looking for a good club to pound the tub with.' She leaned forward. 'What do you have?'

'I'm waiting for the lab reports. I talked to Silver at Bisonte's office and to Laura Kern at the forensics lab out in San Leandro, and all I know for sure is Bjorner's dead. Heck, I knew that yesterday. I want to know what killed him.'

'What about that warning fax? Any progress on tracking down the sender?'

'Nothing.' You never said 'no luck' to Dorothy Yamura. She didn't like coincidences, and she didn't believe in luck at all.

Yamura looked at Marvia, obviously waiting for information.

'I have to study the reports from the people we had at the station. Check the canvass. And I want to interview the next of kin.'

Yamura nodded. 'Who's that?'

'Bjorner had a brother, Herb. I already talked with him at the station last night. He seems cooperative. Upset but fairly coherent. The receptionist at the station says he brought Bob to the studio every afternoon and took him home after his show. Did you know that Bob Bjorner was almost totally blind?'

Yamura sat up straight. 'No.' It was a long, drawn-out no. 'What do you think that means? Is it relevant?'

'No idea. Maybe it's got nothing to do with his death. But he used a Braille script. I want it turned into typescript. I want to know what he was going to say in his last broadcast. I'm going to call UC and get somebody there to read it back for me. And I want to get an air-check from KRED and see if there's anything there.'

Yamura said, 'Sounds good, Marvia. I want to move fast on this, and it looks like you're a step ahead of the game.'

Marvia stood up. 'I'll be happier when I see the reports from the coroner and chem lab.'

'Who's handling it?'

'Gemma Silver says Bisonte's doing the PM himself. And Laura Kern is doing the chem checks at the forensics lab.'

'Keep me posted.'

Marvia headed back to her own desk. She scanned the reports from Holloway, Rosetti and Gutierrez. It looked as if they'd all done their jobs, and it looked as if none of them had learned anything useful.

She padded into the squad room, where she poured herself a cup of coffee and scanned the morning papers. There was an Oakland *Trib* under the creamer and there were copies of both of the San Francisco morning papers, the long-running *Chronicle* and the brash upstart *Mirror*. The *Trib* gave the Bjorner case a tease above the logo on the main news section and a story on page one of the local news section. They had a photo of the body bag on the gurney being loaded into the coroner's ambulance in the KRED parking lot. The *Chron* actually put the story on its front page but used no photo.

KRED KILLER, the main *Mirror* headline read. And the subhead, *Radical 'Caster Croaks into Mike — Was Radio Red's Final Message Cry for Help?* And, would you believe it, they had a photo of the cadaver slumped across the broadcaster's desk in Studio B. They ran it the width of the front page.

How the hell did they get that? There was a credit line on the photo but it just said, *Staff*. The story itself started on page three with another juicy headline and a shot similar to the Oakland *Trib*'s and another — how in bloody blue blazing hell did they get this one? — of Marvia

Plum conversing with Herb Bjorner. You could see Bjorner clearly; he was standing in front of the KRED building. You could see the station call letters on the marquee, and there was a uniformed police officer with her back to the camera, talking with Bjorner. You couldn't see her face, but there was no question it was Marvia Plum. Her sergeant's stripes were even visible.

The story itself was headlined simply, *KRED KILLING*. It was bylined, *Special to the San Francisco Mirror, by Maude Markham.*

Marvia thought she knew most of the local media, by face or by byline if not in person. She'd only been gone for a matter of weeks. But she didn't know Maude Markham. Maybe a new reporter. Maybe a college kid interning at the *Mirror*, who had just got very, very lucky.

She heard a page over the loudspeaker: 'Sergeant Plum, pick up your phone.' The page didn't say who was calling, but Marvia could easily feel the looming presence of city council member Sherry Hanson.

6

There were two buttons blinking on Marvia's telephone, and when she picked up the handset the voice wasn't that of Sherry Hanson but of Herbert Bjorner. He was not happy.

'I didn't give permission to put my picture in the newspaper. Did you arrange that?'

'I just saw it myself. I was as surprised as you, Mr. Bjorner.'

'What's the matter with those vultures, don't they have any respect? My brother is dead!'

'I'm really sorry. But since you phoned — '

'Do you have any information? Who did it? And how?'

'We're still waiting for the coroner's report. We don't know that your brother's death was due to anything other than natural causes. But for the time being, I'm treating Robert's death as a homicide.'

'Robert, is it? Not Radio Red? Not Bolshevik Bob?'

'Mr. Bjorner, I'd like to talk with you. Would it be okay if I come to your house? Would it be convenient if I come over now?'

He seemed surprised. There was a silence, and then he said: 'The bed ain't made and the breakfast dishes ain't washed or nothing.'

'That's really all right. As long as you weren't planning to go out. I'll be over in a little while.'

The second line had gone dark. If it was Sherry Hanson, she could just phone again and Marvia would say she never got the call. Instead of worrying about that, she punched in a number at the University of California computer lab. Soon she was connected with Wilma Ransome. They exchanged greetings, then Marvia said, 'What can you do with Braille?'

'What do you want done?' Ransome always sounded as if she'd just swallowed a tablespoon of honey.

'You hear about the death over at

KRED yesterday?'

'Who hasn't? Biggest thing to hit this town since the National Guard. Besides, I feel as if I have a kind of auntie relationship with KRED.'

'What do you mean?'

'You didn't know? Pete D'Allessandro is my grandpa. He's pretty old, but he still lives in Berkeley.'

'Remind me.' The name sounded familiar.

'He started that station, right after World War Two. Four people — he was one of the founders. What's my role in this little drama, Plum?'

'Bjorner, the victim, was visually challenged.'

'You mean the guy was blind?'

'Some question about that. Apparently he caught some white phosphorus in the face in World War Two and lost most of his sight. But he may have had some vision left.'

'So what's with the Braille?'

'He was in the studio when he died, about to go on the air. He had a script with him, typed in Braille. I can't read it.'

'And you want me to tell you what it says? I can't read the stuff myself very well; it's obsolescent, what with talking books and microcassettes. I learned it when I was a kid but I hardly ever use it. And nowadays you can't get 'em to study it. The kids all say they want talking books, they correspond by tape, and they think there's a miracle coming any day now to give 'em eyes.'

'So what can you do for me?'

'Okay, just between us girls, I've been working with Fabia Rabinowitz. We've got a machine that can read Braille and convert it into any format you want — text file, printer, voice synthesizer, whatever. Sounds like Stephen Hawking reading the morning newspaper. Or go the other way — scan a document or start with a file and turn it into Braille. Neat gadget. Fabia thinks it's a trivial problem; didn't challenge her swollen, throbbing brain. But it's going to be very useful. And we've got the prototype up and running.'

'Great! I'll have to check Bjorner's last script out of the evidence room. I'd rather photocopy it and keep the original locked up, but I guess that wouldn't do.'

'Sure wouldn't. See you later, hey?'

* * *

Herbert Bjorner's house was on Vine Street. It came straight out of a 1940s film noir: gray stucco walls carved into rounded arches; a shaded veranda with metal furniture on it. The whole thing was set back from the roadway, raised twenty feet above street level with a sloping lawn and a row of California palm trees that hid the house.

The sky was gray and the air was cold and damp. Marvia shivered in her red sweatshirt as she trudged up the stairs to the house. She pressed the doorbell. After a long wait, Herbert Bjorner answered the door. He was wearing what looked like a union suit made of heavy cotton that might once have been white, but was now yellowed with time. It buttoned up the front but it was collarless. Over the lower half he had pulled a pair of nondescript tan pants. He wore tattered slippers.

He glared at Marvia. 'You're her, all right. Come on.' He stood aside so she could walk past him. 'You going to give Bob back to me?' Bjorner asked. 'I get to bury him, don't I?'

'I thought — I'm sorry, Mr. Bjorner. The coroner has to perform an autopsy. In fact, when we leave here, it would be a good idea for me to drive you down to Oakland so you can identify him.'

'Christ, Sergeant, the man is dead. We know who he is.'

'It's just a formality.'

Bjorner pointed a puffy hand and Marvia made her way into what had to be the living room. It had a high beamed ceiling and a smooth stone floor; a fireplace that looked as if it hadn't been used in years; tall windows with heavy, dust-drenched drapes; heavy wooden furniture; and dark, worn upholstery. On this gray morning it felt like night.

Marvia sat opposite Bjorner. He was on the couch, and she faced him from a heavy wooden chair. He offered her coffee and set two cups on the table between them. She took a sip, more to be polite than because she wanted it.

'Do you mind if I tape our conversation, Mr. Bjorner?' She expected easy agreement, but he tilted his head and stared at her out of a half-closed eye.

'None of that 'you have the right to remain silent' crap?'

She had already set the recorder on the table, but she hadn't turned it on. 'Mr. Bjorner, you don't have to talk to me if you don't want to.'

'I'm not a suspect?'

'No, sir.'

'I don't need a lawyer?'

'Call one if you wish. But really, I'm just trying to get some information. I want to solve this thing; find out what happened to your brother. Don't you?'

He finally agreed, and Marvia read the date and address into the recorder's condenser mike, then asked Bjorner to ID himself for the record.

'Do you know anyone who would want to kill your brother? I'm operating on the assumption that he was murdered. If it turns out that he died of natural causes, I'll just scrub my investigation.'

Bjorner considered. 'The right would have loved to put him out of the way.'

'The right?'

'The fascists. Neo-Nazis. KKK.'

Marvia nodded. 'Right, I understand. Was there anyone in particular? Did Robert get into any quarrels that you know of? Did he receive any threatening telephone calls or letters?'

'He did at KRED.'

So Herb Bjorner knew about the fax message that had arrived at KRED the previous afternoon. Or did he? Marvia had taken the fax from Sun Mbolo; when she skimmed the newspaper reports of Robert's death there had been no mention of the warning. But everybody at the station knew about it. If Marvia had been able to hold that message back, it might have been useful. But it was already too late when she'd gotten there.

'When did he receive the most recent threat?'

Herb Bjorner shook his head. 'They used to come in all the time. I don't know when he got the last one.'

'Did he save them?'

'Oh, Bob was an archivist. He had all his scripts, going back to the '50s. Everything is in file cabinets.'

'All in Braille?' Marvia asked.

'No, he used to type 'em out. He wasn't blind, you know. He caught a splash of white phosphorus in the eyes on Tarawa. He was a big, tough marine. Had to pass for white to get into the corps — they didn't want us then. Not in combat, that's for sure. Give 'em guns and train 'em to use the things and what do you think they'll do with 'em? Talk about patriotism. We tried to enlist together to fight the Nazis, but he wound up in the Marine Corps in the Pacific and I wound up at Port Chicago loading supply ships.'

He set his coffee cup back beside the tape recorder without taking a sip. 'November 20, 1943. I got off shift at the base and headed for the pay phone. I'd had the creepiest feeling all day and knew something had happened. Bob used to write letters, but they couldn't tell you much; couldn't tell you where they was or what was really happening. But everybody read the newspapers and listened to the radio, so we knew what was coming. When the Marines landed on Tarawa, I knew they were going to get the crap pounded out of them. And they did. My dad answered the phone. You ever see his picture?'

He didn't wait for a reply, but crossed to the fireplace and returned with an eight-by-ten photo that had been hand-tinted. It was mounted in a cheap gold-leaf frame and showed a couple in their best Sunday outfits, the man in a brown pinstripe suit and fedora, the woman in a dark dress and round picture hat. The man was white and the woman was black.

Marvia looked at Herbert Bjorner and nodded.

Bjorner said, 'They got a telegram from the Navy Department saying that Bob was wounded on Tarawa and was being returned to Pearl Harbor to the hospital. They saved his eyes, some. But later they just got worse and worse and they couldn't do nothing about it. He got a disability pension, and he kept going back to the vets' hospital, but they couldn't help him none. He finally switched to Braille.'

He rubbed his own eyes as if the gesture would put him into communion with his dead brother. 'You know how many casualties they took in that fight? The landing craft got hung up on the reef and our guys had to wade in to the beach. That was the planning of the wonderful Admiral Turner. I know it by heart, Sergeant. We sent in 4,700 Marines and we took 3,178 casualties, dead and wounded. I've studied that battle, believe me. The enemy had 5,000 defenders on Tarawa, and when the fight was over we took the survivors prisoner. Seventeen men. Seventeen. All the rest was dead. I guess I admire their courage, but you have to say those guys was plain crazy.'

'But the threats,' Marvia interrupted.

'Bob enrolled at Cal after the war, after they let him out of the hospital. They sent him back from Hawaii to Letterman in San Francisco, then over to Oakland so's he'd be close to home. When KRED started broadcasting he was very excited.

He'd done some radio work before the war. He paid more attention to school than me. We was just kids, but it was still new in those days, pretty new anyway, and you could get a start. After the war, when they started KRED, he got a job there. They called him staff announcer. He got into that analyst thing later on, when the cold war was so intense. You wouldn't remember that, would you, Officer? How old are you?'

Marvia said, 'Old enough. I was in the army, in Germany. I don't remember the whole cold war, but I remember enough of it.'

'Well, the government started shipping matériel out to the Pacific again from Concord. Matériel — nukes, you know. They never admitted it, but everybody knowed it was nukes. That was during Korea. Bob could still see some then. We went out to Concord together; got arrested a couple times. Then during Vietnam it was even worse. And the stuff at Cal — riots, the National Guard and the tear gas. Was you in Berkeley then?'

'I was a kid.'

'Everything got what they call polarized. I took Bob to People's Park. He had KRED press papers. His eyes was still working some. They didn't care. He got clubbed and gassed and arrested. They used to talk about people getting radicalized. Huh!'

Marvia pursed her lips. 'I understand Bob's position. Politically, I mean. He *was* Radio Red, after all.'

Herb Bjorner smiled.

'Were there any others in the family?' Marvia asked.

'Mother died in '55. Dad just lost interest after that. He was a healthy man, but he just lost interest and he died within the year.'

'Did you have any other brothers or sisters?'

Bjorner shook his head. 'Just Bob and me. Now it's just me. He was with a wonderful woman, you know. Got together in — wait a minute . . . yes, 1951. Beautiful girl. Taught school in Emeryville. Never had no children. She died, too, in 1980. I lived here all the time. Stayed here when Mom died, stayed here when Dad died.

Bob and Anitra, that was her name — very exotic, eh? Bob and Anitra, they had a house down in Emeryville near her school. When she died, Bob moved back in here with me.'

He looked up at her as if a surprising thought had occurred to him. 'Radio Red. Bob had red hair, you know. Used to. Not now. That was why they called him Radio Red, back in '39, '40 when he was getting started. Worked at KPO and KSAN, the old KSAN on AM, not that one they got now. He had red hair and freckles. I don't think they knew about . . . '

He picked up the framed photo again, of his and Robert's parents. 'Bob was light-complected with freckles and red hair. So was I, for that matter. He wouldn't have got hired if they knew. And Bjorner, they wondered why he looked like an Irishman instead of a blond Swede, but they liked him. He was a talented guy, even when he was a kid. Could talk up a storm; read a script first time through so's you'd think it was coming straight out of his head; read a commercial so's you thought he was your next-door neighbor just telling you about something he bought today. Radio Red.'

Marvia said, 'Enemies. Or close friends. Tell me about people he knew.'

'They used to give away radios, too. Bet you didn't know that. Wait right here.' He stood up and disappeared through a doorway. Marvia turned off the tape recorder.

Bjorner returned carrying a plastic radio not much bigger than a camera. He held it toward Marvia. 'Go on, take it. Hasn't played in years. Bob never threw nothing away.'

Marvia accepted the radio. It couldn't have weighed more than a pound and a half. It was molded of bright red plastic; the color hadn't faded. There were just two knobs on the front, for volume and for tuning. The tuning dial was marked with FM frequencies; and at the place where KRED transmitted its signal, there was a copy of the station's logo, the letters picked out in lightning bolts.

'Nobody had FM back then.' Bjorner reached out and petted the radio as Marvia held it, as if it were a kitten he had handed her and he wanted to make sure it wasn't frightened. 'Nobody had FM, so they cut a deal with some outfit down by San Jose, I don't know who, probably making computers now. They made these little radios for KRED, and KRED ran ads in the newspapers: if you subscribed to KRED, they'd send you a free radio to listen to it on.'

'That work?' Marvia asked.

'Must have. Station didn't go off the air.'

Marvia handed the little radio back. 'Good point.' Bjorner set it down on the table next to the picture of his parents. After his initial suspicion he seemed to be enjoying the show-and-tell session.

Marvia asked, 'Who typed his scripts for him in Braille?'

Bjorner seemed surprised. 'Nobody. He had a Braille typewriter. He did it all himself.'

Marvia had turned the tape recorder back on when Bjorner started talking again. She thought of asking Herb for all his brother's scripts. The older ones she could read, and the more recent Wilma

Ransome could translate. But that would be a huge and time-consuming task. It could go on for months and it might lead nowhere. For now, she was going to have Wilma convert only the script from Bjorner's fatal broadcast, the script he had never delivered. That might provide a clue.

'Mr. Bjorner, I want to ask you once more about even casual acquaintances of your brother. What about your neighbors here on Vine Street? Did Robert get along with them? Did he ever quarrel with anyone? Ever get into political discussions?'

Herbert shook his head. 'He went to meetings and rallies. Bob was committed to the movement. He didn't have time for no social niceties. He used to listen to the radio; listened to some of those right-wing thugs and then call them and set them straight when they mucked up the facts, which they do all the time in case you don't happen to know that. He could be testy. But not face to face, not in the neighborhood.'

Marvia shut off the tape recorder. She

slipped it into her pocket and thanked Bjorner for his help. 'If you'll come with me now, I can give you a ride down to the coroner's office. I'll have to stay there for the autopsy, but I can arrange a ride home for you.'

'You're going to stay for the autopsy? That must be a grisly business.' Bjorner shivered. 'Do they have to do one? Can't they just bury my brother?'

'No. There's suspicion of foul play, so the law requires that we determine cause of death. And I have to attend. I'm the officer in charge of this case. It's procedure.'

'I can take the Oldsmobile.'

'You might not wish to drive afterwards. This can be a very upsetting experience for next of kin.'

'I can handle it. I'll follow you down there. You're going now, right? Just give me a minute and I'll follow you in the Oldsmobile.'

'If you insist.'

'You won't do anything,' Bjorner said.

'What?'

'You won't do anything. Look at you.'

He held out his hand and pressed it against Marvia's. 'You're my African sister and you've sold out to the bosses and their power structure. They're just as happy that Radio Red won't be a thorn in their side no more. Aren't you ashamed of yourself, my African sister?'

Marvia said, 'Thank you for your assistance, Mr. Bjorner.'

She started down the staircase that led to the street, then turned around and saw Bjorner standing in the open doorway, watching her. She was getting soaked by the rain. She said, 'How did your brother get up and down these steps? How do you?'

Bjorner said, 'There's an elevator to the garage.'

Marvia sat in her cruiser waiting for Bjorner to take the elevator down to his garage and follow her in the huge battered Oldsmobile. They seemed a perfect match: The man and the car were both old and overweight and not really working very well anymore.

7

Robert Bjorner didn't really look so bad, for a corpse. The scarlet coloring had receded from his face as the body began its postmortem processes. Rigor set in, and blood drained toward the center of gravity. He was laid out on a table, and Herbert Bjorner viewed the body on a video monitor. Coroners had gone to that system in recent years. It was less stressful for families; there were fewer scenes of hysterical grief or misdirected rage.

The coroner's office was located on Fourth Street in Oakland, near OPD headquarters and the city jail and courthouse. It was cop heaven. Marvia half-expected to run into her old friend Phil High, but she hoped she wouldn't. High would be sure to ask her about Bart Lindsey, and she just didn't want to talk about him today.

Marvia showed her ID at the door and was admitted. Inside the building,

Gemma Silver displayed Robert Bjorner's body for his brother, who nodded and wiped away tears. Marvia had not found him the pleasantest or most helpful of men, but she felt sympathy for him.

Herb Bjorner said, 'Yes. No question, that's Bobby.'

He signed the form putting his verification on record, then asked when he could have his brother back. He was going to have him buried in a national cemetery. As much as Bobby detested American policies and actions, he still loved his country, and Herb intended to claim Robert's rights as an honorably discharged veteran.

Silver told him that the autopsy was scheduled for that afternoon. Normal procedure was to hold whatever materials were needed for evidence and release the remains promptly.

Bjorner nodded. He stood gazing at the video monitor, then said, 'I'll get to look at him again before the funeral.' No one disagreed. 'I'll go home now.' He turned to Marvia. 'Is that all right?'

'Of course.' She checked her watch and

decided to catch a bite of lunch. She left her cruiser at the curb and walked up to Mexicali Rose and ate a burrito, then walked back to the coroner's office. Now she stood in the workroom, surgical greens and gauze mask over her sweat-shirt and jeans, and watched Edgar Bisonte earn his salary.

Speaking into a tape recorder, with a video camera recording his every move, Bisonte noted the condition of the cadaver, from the ruined eyes to the enlarged heart, the damaged lungs, the fatty deposits distributed throughout the body cavity, the partially decayed liver. The brain appeared normal, as did the extremities. The contents of the stomach were removed for microscopic, chemical, and toxicological examination. Blood had already been drained from the cadaver, and a sample was also included in the materials for analysis.

Soon Marvia sat in Bisonte's office, listening to his preliminary comments. 'Beats the daylights out of me.' Bisonte blinked once and steepled his fingers. He'd doffed his surgical greens and slipped into the jacket of a handsome business suit. He placed his fingertips on a thin sheaf of papers and cocked his head to look at the top sheet. 'Mr. Bjorner wasn't in very good shape. At his age, and with the problems he was suffering, I doubt he would have lived another five years. Probably much less.'

'But what killed him?'

'I told you, Sergeant. Beats the daylights out of me.'

Marvia said, 'Is *that* what you're going to report, Dr. Bisonte? That's going to be the official cause of death?'

'We won't put it quite that way, Sergeant, but that's essentially it. Unless the lab report tells me something. Certainly there was no sign of violence, no trauma. Something very nasty happened to his face and eyes, but that was a long time ago. I saw no ruptured blood vessels. We look for coronary or cerebral hemorrhage, embolism, occlusion in a case like this. I found none. No evidence of malignancy.'

'You're telling me that he just stopped living.'

'In effect, yes.'

'What about poison?'

'Ah-hah! Good work, Sergeant Plum! The victim was poisoned, possibly by the injection of the venom of the Egyptian cobra, administered by coating a needle-thin icicle delivered via blowpipe through a ventilating grille in the ceiling of the KRED radio studio. Very nice.'

Marvia said, 'I'll need a copy of your official report for the case file. And when will you have the lab work-ups on his blood and stomach contents?'

'How urgent is this?'

Marvia tried to make him understand. She almost whispered, 'Very.'

'I can phone something over in a day, or have one of my people do it. Full work-up takes a long time, but we'll try to get you something fast.'

*   *   *

Marvia retrieved her cruiser and took the freeway back to Berkeley. She took the exit ramp at University Avenue and parked in Northside, then made her way

104

to the UC computer lab. The lab was located in an eye-wrenchingly ugly new building on Hearst Avenue, but the inside of the building was functional and nobody seemed to be complaining about the exterior.

Marvia carried a briefcase containing Robert Bjorner's final Radio Red script, still sealed in its evidence envelope. She had to show her ID to get into the building. Everybody was getting security-conscious these days.

Wilma Ransome and Fabia Rabinowitz shared a double cubicle, ergonomic desks furnished with high-powered Circuitron workstations. Rabinowitz's workstation was topped by an oversized monitor. Ransome's had an odd-looking keyboard and a pair of speakers.

Marvia had known Rabinowitz for years, having worked with her on earlier cases. It was the tall, stately Rabinowitz with her wavy blue-black hair who had introduced Marvia to the shorter, comfortable-looking Ransome. Her blonde hair and brown eyes were striking. Ransome had formed the habit of following

105

conversations by the sound of voices, looking at the speaker. It took a while to realize that she was blind.

When Marvia entered the office, she announced herself. Ransome turned and asked if she'd brought the script. Marvia opened the envelope. 'It's been checked for fingerprints. Just Bjorner's, so don't worry about that. But it's still evidence. You'll have to sign for it and keep it locked up.'

Ransome tilted her head toward a file cabinet with a rotary lock on the top drawer. 'That do? I'm the only one who knows the combination.'

Marvia nodded her assent and handed the envelope to Ransome. Ransome signed — Marvia guided her hand to a line on the envelope — and Marvia entered the rest of the information and initialed next to Ransome's signature.

'Okay, Marvia, just tell me what you want. This is the infamous Radio Red's farewell address to the world, hey?'

'I just want a printout of the text. Straight conversion.'

'Piece of cake. Give me twenty-four

hours; should be plenty.'

Minutes later, back at the Hall of Justice, Marvia carried a cup of coffee back to her desk and looked at the messages that had arrived since morning. The call slip from her nemesis on the city council seemed to pulse with an evil light. She sighed and picked it up, reread it, then dialed city hall.

Council member Sherry Hanson didn't waste time on pleasantries. 'What are you doing about Radio Red?'

'Following procedure.' Marvia had long since stopped trying to make nice with Hanson.

'I spoke with the chief, you know. I want security for KRED. It's an invaluable community asset. I want that murder solved, and I want that station and the people who work there to feel safe.'

'Ms. Hanson, did someone tell you there was a murder at KRED?'

'Certainly.'

'That's news to me. I know there was a death there yesterday. Last I knew, we were still waiting for the autopsy and lab reports.' She looked up at the wall clock, wondering how long before she had a call from Edgar Bisonte — or more likely Gemma Silver — with a preliminary report on the blood and stomach work-ups, or from Forensics with a work-up on the ashtray leavings and the food containers that had been removed from Studio B after Bjorner's death.

Sherry Hanson said, 'You know, some of us urged Oceana to put a uniformed guard on the door at KRED, but they wouldn't do it: 'We're open to the public, we're part of the community, we can't shut ourselves off like the big stations.' And that awful Mbolo woman they've got running the place, turning it into nothing but a clone of the trash broadcasters. Next thing, I expect them to start running commercials.'

Marvia made a noncommittal sound. Hanson was rattling on: ' . . . half a century of service to the community, and I'm preparing a resolution to present in the city council, expressing our outrage at the heinous crime. I'm going to move that we direct the Police Review Commission to investigate possible involvement by the police department, or at least negligence and dereliction of duty, and blah-blah-blah . . . '

'Ms. Hanson, we're not even sure that there was a crime committed. If there was, we'll treat this case, if it *was* a homicide, like any homicide — whether the victim is a homeless person sleeping in the park or the highest official in city hall.'

'I want you to keep me informed.'

Marvia said, 'Yes, ma'am,' and replaced the receiver. They'd clashed repeatedly over the years, Hanson pushing an agenda based on the politics that made Berkeley run. The politics of race, class and sex. She'd singled out Marvia Plum early in Marvia's career. A black female cop with a working-class background must have looked like an ideal protégée for the ambitious Sherry Hanson, and at first Marvia had responded to the favorable attention from city hall. But soon Marvia realized that Hanson was using her as a mole in the Hall of Justice, inviting her to friendly little meetings and pumping her for inside PD gossip. There was never a real explosion between them; instead, Marvia had backed away, delayed answering Hanson's phone calls, ignored her so-politically-correct suggestions, and followed department protocol to the letter. It had saved her career, she thought. And she was certain that it had saved her self-respect. But it had won her an enemy in city hall.

Scanning the papers on her desk, Marvia shook her head. She jotted a note on her calendar so she'd remember to keep after Edgar Bisonte and Laura Kern. And she'd have to follow up with Wilma Ransome at the computer lab and find out what Radio Red had planned to say in his last broadcast. Another thought bubbled to the surface, and she made a note to talk with Sun Mbolo once more. Was there an air-check going at the time of Bjorner's death? Even if Bjorner hadn't actually gone on the air, could his studio engineer have started a tape rolling? Marvia would have to find out who Bjorner's engineer was, and pursue that issue.

Once Bjorner's death was ruled a

homicide — or a probable homicide — Marvia would convene as many people involved in the case as she could for a brainstorming session: certainly the uniforms who had been at KRED that afternoon, questioning the station staff; as well as the evidence techs, Ransome and Kern, and Bisonte or Silver. Maybe she'd also invite Dorothy Yamura. Yamura had been Marvia's friend and her sponsor in the BPD ever since Marvia was a rookie cop and Yamura her watch commander. Would inviting Yamura to the brainstorm be a sign that Marvia was unsure of herself, and that she was trying to buck Sherry Hanson's heat back up the line? Well, she'd sleep on that tonight. Once the brainstorm was convened, Marvia and the other participants would review the sequence of events, rolling time backwards from the discovery of the body to the moment of death and beyond, to the act that brought about Bob Bjorner's death. They would find out how Bjorner was killed, and why he was killed, and finally they would find out by whom he was killed.

8

Jamie was sitting on the veranda when Marvia pulled the Mustang into the driveway. He was wearing his Oakland Raiders cap, a black T-shirt and black jeans. The line from his headphones ran to a portable CD player that he was holding on his lap. He stared straight ahead until Marvia had climbed the steps to the veranda.

Marvia hadn't got away from McKinley Avenue until after eight o'clock. Gloria and Jamie would probably have eaten by now, and Gloria would have her eyes glued to the TV and the telephone glued to her ear. Marvia put her hands gently on the sides of her son's face, hoping to get a smile from him. He stared stonily ahead.

'What's the matter, Jamie?'

He reached slowly with one hand to raise his Raiders cap, used the other to slide the headphones back, then replaced the cap. 'You know,' he said accusingly.

Marvia felt a chill. She'd ordered him to come straight home from school, and told him she would phone to check on him. But she hadn't called.

'I was in Oakland. I was in an autopsy workroom. You wouldn't have liked it, Jamie.'

'You didn't call.'

'I couldn't, Jamie. I was conducting a homicide investigation.'

'You promised.'

She felt a pang. She had made a pledge to him, and she had failed him. 'I'm sorry, Jamie.'

'You think you can tell me what to do, you think you're so perfect, and you can't even keep a promise.'

She tried to think of a reply.

'You go whoring off with that dirty old man and you leave me here with that mean bitch.'

Marvia gasped and recoiled, then saw the tears in her son's eyes finally spill over. She grabbed him and held him to her, feeling hot wetness on the side of her neck. What had she been thinking? He was right, and she didn't know how to apologize and make it better.

She inhaled. 'Want to go out for dinner? Did you eat anything?' By this time of night she expected that he had, but he shook his head. 'Chinese or Mexican?' she offered.

Jamie sat like a statue, then deliberately removed his headphones and shut off the CD player.

'Will you wait for me, Jamie?' He nodded. She went inside and found Gloria exactly where she expected to find her. Over the sound of some ancient music video, Marvia said, 'I'm taking Jamie out for food. You want anything?'

Gloria looked up at Marvia, shook her head vigorously, and turned her eyes back to the TV.

Marvia sighed and went back onto the veranda. On the way she grabbed a lightweight jacket and slipped it on over her sweatshirt. Jamie was standing beside the driveway. When Marvia reached him he said, 'Better lock the Discman in the trunk if you don't want a smashed window.' She slipped her arm around his shoulders. Somehow his words were precious to her.

They drove into Oakland and parked in Chinatown, left the Mustang in a garage and climbed the stairs to a second-story restaurant on Webster Street. It was bright and noisy. Most of the diners were Asian. Near the kitchen was a salt-water aquarium, a big one, with puffers and blue-and-yellow tangs and striped Moorish idols darting around like living rocket ships or drifting peacefully like orbiting space stations.

A waiter carried menus to their table. 'Beverage?'

Marvia would have loved a Tsingtao, but she said, 'Tea. Jamie?'

'Just water.'

They ate their appetizers, then shared soup and an order of spiced prawns and a veggie stirfry. Conversation was difficult. Jamie's outburst seemed to have helped him, though Marvia knew that she had not given him any real explanation. But for now she had to do something about the problem with Hakeem White. Smoking a joint might be a two-bit matter, but

Jamie and Hakeem were consorting with dangerous characters. She asked what Jamie knew about Blue Beetle and Acid Alice.

He picked up a spicy prawn with a pair of chopsticks. When he'd swallowed he said, 'If you had a beer, Mom, I'd borrow a sip right now. That's *hot*.'

Marvia resisted the bait. She lifted her teacup and sipped carefully, waiting for more from her son.

'All right. Are you asking as my mom or as a cop?'

'As your mother. Just talk to me, Jamie. I know I'm not around as much as you'd like, and I'm sorry, truly. But now is your chance.'

'They call him Blue Beetle 'cause he has one tattooed on his cheek. It's kind of creepy but it's really neat, too. And Alice is really nice-looking, even if she's kind of ancient . . . at least twenty-five. Maybe even thirty!'

Marvia nodded. 'What else?'

'He's a black dude — light-complected, though, so you can see the tattoo on his face. Real short dreadlocks. Dresses like a regular brother — you know, T-shirts, baggies, sneakers.'

Marvia had seen the man on Telegraph Avenue near the main entryway to the University of California.

'Alice, I don't know. She has kind of sharp features, green eyes, long crinkly hair past her shoulders. She likes to wear these nice tops.' He ran a finger across his chest.

'So you can see her breasts.' *God help me, how do I talk about women's bodies with my pre-pubescent son?* 'So you don't see much else about her, and she keeps your attention while Blue Beetle transacts business.'

'Um, I guess so.'

'What do they sell, Jamie?'

'Anything. Ganja, hash, crystal, blow, horse.'

'Crack?

Jamie looked back at his plate. 'I guess so.'

'What else besides drugs? Do they sell guns?'

Jamie nodded reluctantly.

'I won't betray you, Jamie, but would

you talk to a friend of mine, please?'

'Who's that?'

'Inspector Stillman. He's a cop.'

Now she could see fear in her son's face. She said, 'I promise nothing will happen to you. I won't tell him who it is until I get his pledge of confidentiality, and that nothing will happen to you. Or Hakeem.'

'Or my other friends.'

'Jamie, we're not interested in busting kids. We want to get the dealers. If I know Stillman, he won't even be very interested in Blue Beetle or Acid Alice. He'll want to get the people who supply them with the drugs and the guns. Are there guns in your school, Jamie?'

He shrugged. 'You're carrying one, Mom. I know that. Don't try to hide it from me.'

'I have to carry it, Jamie. It's my job.'

'It's still a gun.'

'All right, Jamie. Thank you. Want to order more food?'

He shook his head no. She looked around for their waiter, then signaled for their check. She saw two people she knew eating at a table near the aquarium. When she had paid for their dinner, they headed toward the exit. Marvia stopped to introduce her son to Wilma Ransome and Fabia Rabinowitz.

Wilma said, 'Marvia, I'm glad we ran into you. There were a few glitches with that conversion, but Fabia lent me a hand and it looks pretty good. I think I can get a file done in the morning and print it out for you anytime you want. Or I could just modem it to you.'

'No, I'll have to get back the Braille version. I'll come by in the morning. Should I call first?'

'Just come by. If I'm not at my desk they'll just reel in my tether.' She smiled broadly. 'So nice to meet you, Jamie.'

* * *

Marvia found a memo on her desk in the morning. Inspector Mack Stillman would like to chat concerning the two subjects she had inquired about. She dialed his extension, found that he was at his desk, and asked if she could come

119

right over. He said sure.

Stillman had a rep as a square shooter, and he had the physique to go with it. He looked up at Marvia and nodded. He minced no words. 'What's with Beetle and Alice, Sergeant?'

'Confidential source, right, Inspector? I gave my word, and I have to keep it.'

'Sure. Have a seat. Tell me what you have to tell me.'

'My source says that Blue Beetle and Acid Alice are dealing to some pretty young kids. Benjamin Banneker Junior High. And they're peddling guns, too.'

Stillman jerked erect. 'To Banneker kids? That's a good school, good neighborhood. We haven't had any reports out of there.'

Marvia held her silence.

'What are they dealing? What kind of dope and how much of it? And — guns?' He shook his head dazedly. 'What the hell is wrong with our guys? We should have known this. Come on, Sergeant, give. Details.'

'I came across a couple of kids smoking jays, Inspector. Not much to it. I started to scold them. One of them clammed up but the other one felt like talking. Next thing I knew I had names. The kid gave me a list of drugs. The usual street stuff, no surprises. I figured a good talking-to for sonny boy and I'd check with you about Beetle and Alice. And then he gives me the gun report. Out of the blue.' That was close enough to the truth to keep Marvia's conscience calm if not happy.

'You don't want to give me your source?' Stillman said.

'I'll ask the kid if he'll talk to you. I know where he lives.'

'Right.' Stillman nodded. 'You have a son, don't you, Sergeant? Didn't you bring him in here one time to see the place? Polite young fellow. How old would he be?'

Marvia checked her wristwatch and rose abruptly. 'I have a meet. Look, Inspector, what are you going to do about Beetle and Alice?'

'Secondhand report from an anonymous juvenile is hardly probable cause. But I'll try and get an undercover to make a buy. Something more than a bag of grass, eh? See if I can get a warrant for Beetle and Alice's home sweet home, wherever it is this week.' He stood up. 'Work on your source, Sergeant. If he'll help me out, he can wear my cop hat and I'll buy him an ice-cream cone.'

Marvia checked out a cruiser and headed for the UC computer lab in Northside. She parked and found Wilma Ransome and Fabia Rabinowitz's cubicle. When she stood in the doorway, Ransome turned her uncanny sightless brown eyes on her. 'Morning, Marvia.'

Marvia said her good mornings to both women. 'Everything set on that printout?'

'Easy as pie.' Ransome stood up and put her hand on the secure file cabinet. She didn't hesitate or feel her way; she knew every inch of this office. She spun the dial on the combination lock, then reached in and removed Radio Red's last Braille script, neatly sealed back in the evidence envelope, as well as a computer printout. She turned back and held the papers for Marvia. They checked the documents and completed the paper-work.

Marvia said, 'I want to get back to work and read this script. Did you get any feel for what Bjorner was planning to talk about that last day?'

Ransome shook her head. 'I only paid attention to the coding and the conversion.'

'Right. BPD and UC will settle for your time charges, okay?'

*   *   *

Back at the Hall of Justice, Marvia returned the envelope and Bjorner's Braille script to Evidence, then settled in at her desk and started reading the printout.

Comrades — After Stalin's death, the Central Committee of the party began to implement a policy explaining concisely and consistently that it is impermissible and foreign to the spirit of Marxism-Leninism to elevate one person, to transform him into a superman possessing supernatural characteristics akin to those of a god. Such a man supposedly knows everything; sees everything; thinks for everyone;

can do anything; is infallible in his behavior.

Nobody talked liked that. It just didn't sound like even a KRED radical. More like the tripe Marvia used to hear in Germany, when they'd sit around after hours listening to the GDR radio spouting gobbledygook and laugh at it.

Such a belief about a man, and specifically about Stalin, was cultivated among us for many years. In December, 1922, in a letter to the Party Congress, Vladimir Ilyich wrote, 'After taking over the position of Secretary-General, Comrade Stalin accumulated in his hands immeasurable power, and I am not certain whether he will be always able to use this power with the required care.'

This letter — a political document of tremendous importance known in the party history as Lenin's 'testament' — was distributed to the delegates of the twentieth Party Congress. You have read it, and will undoubtedly read it again more than once. You might reflect on Lenin's plain words, in which expression is given to his anxiety concerning the party, the people, the state, and the future direction of party policy.

Vladimir Ilyich said, 'Stalin is excessively rude, and this defect, which can be freely tolerated in our midst and in contacts among us communists, becomes a defect which cannot be tolerated in one holding the position of the Secretary-General.'

That was all Marvia could take. The style was all too familiar, and she didn't need a time machine to take her back to her army days. But this was attacking Stalin. Somebody had to know what it was. She closed her eyes and concentrated.

She picked up the phone, called Benjamin Banneker Junior High School, and asked for Mr. Florio, the assistant principal. She remembered him running for Berkeley city council once, only to be defeated by Marvia's nemesis, Sherry Hanson.

She read the opening paragraphs of the printout, and Florio said he knew exactly what she was reading. 'It's Comrade Khrushchev's address to the Twentieth Congress of the Communist Party of the USSR. It's the so-called 'secret speech' of 25 February, 1956.'

Marvia blinked. 'You lost me, Ed.'

'It's the famous exposé of Stalin's crimes. Many believe that it was the beginning of the downfall of communism — that it led to Gorbachev and the counterrevolution of '89, the dissolution of the Soviet Union, and the return of capitalism and bourgeois democracy in Russia. There are those who believe that Nikita Khrushchev was himself a CIA plant.'

Marvia tried to keep her head from spinning. 'Ed, please, what does it mean?'

'Where did you come across this, Marvia?'

She told him about Bob Bjorner's script.

'Oh, Radio Red. I saw the pictures in the paper. Heard that KRED was running to the right as fast as that new station manager could scamper. You think she was going to can Bjorner?'

'Please, Ed. About the script.'

'Right. Marvia, it's nothing but Khrushchev's speech, the Cult of Personality speech. Don't you see how it fits?'

'Help me.'

'You know Bob was an old-time radical. He loved metaphors. Bjorner was accusing that new station manager — what's her name?'

'Sun Mbolo.'

' — of creating a cult of personality at KRED. You know, 'keep radio educational and democratic.' That's hardly being democratic, is it, dumping Radio Red after so many years?'

'I see. Thanks for the insight into this Khrushchev thing. And I may drop in on you one day to talk about conditions at BenBan?'

'Anytime, Marvia.'

She hung up and scanned the rest of Bjorner's script. It was more of the same; there seemed nothing new, once you got the general drift. Translate Khrushchev's attack on Stalin to Bjorner's attack on Sun Mbolo. Translate Khrushchev's charges of Stalin's crimes against the party and the party faithful into Bjorner's charges of Sun Mbolo's crimes against KRED and its faithful staffers, and it all made sense.

It sounded almost — *almost* — like a motive for murder, if Bjorner had murdered Mbolo. But nobody had harmed Mbolo. And Bjorner wasn't a suspect; he was the victim. And it had yet to be established that he had been murdered at all. On the other hand, if Bjorner had been murdered, and if Sun Mbolo knew about the script Bjorner was planning to read on his program on KRED, then Mbolo became the suspect.

Marvia's phone rang and she picked up to hear the voice of Laura Kern at the forensics lab.

9

'I've got a prelim for you, Sergeant.'

'Let me have it quick.' Marvia grabbed a pencil and a memo pad.

'First the ashtray. The materials included four burned matches, a matchbook from which six matches had been removed, a small quantity of ash, and two marijuana cigarette butts. We determined that the ashes came from the cigarettes.'

Marvia was jotting notes as Laura Kern spoke.

'We analyzed the cigarettes. The rolling paper was Zig-Zag brand.'

Marvia sniffed. That was a common brand among both dopers and roll-your-own tobacco users. You could buy a package of Zig-Zag papers in half a dozen stores within walking distance of KRED. Hmm. Bob Bjorner, grossly overweight and almost blind, was unlikely to do much walking. But it might be worth following up with Bjorner's brother, Herb. She jotted a note.

'Contents of the cigarette are interesting,' the technician continued. 'Main ingredient is good-quality *Cannabis sativa* flowers with a very high THC content. Probably a mixture of Humboldt Gold and Santa Marta Perfecto, although it's hard to be precise. There were also several pinhead cubes of hashish distributed through the length of the cigarettes. And most interestingly, a trace spiking of cocaine and heroin.'

Marvia straightened. 'Cocaine *and* heroin?'

'That's right, Sergeant.'

Marvia shook her head. 'What a cocktail! Humboldt, Perfecto, hash, and powdered speedball. My God, no wonder it killed him. Who did he think he was, John Belushi?'

'Hold on, Sergeant! I don't really think the joints were a lethal mixture. I mean, based on the length of the roaches and the dimensions of the Zig-Zag rolling papers, and also taking into account the volume of ash that was found — that's assuming he hadn't smoked another joint before this one — I don't think this would have killed a man. Not the amount of chemicals he would have inhaled from three or four small hits off each joint, maybe two big ones. Not knowing his habits, of course.'

'So what are you telling me?'

Laura Kern shuffled papers on her desk. 'The subject may have enjoyed a drug cocktail. He also enjoyed an interesting mixture of ingredients in his food. We found three light cardboard containers marked 'Bara Miyako, 1939 Barbara Jordan Boulevard, Berkeley, California 94704.' One container held a so-called California Roll sushi, intact. The second shows indications of having been filled with boiled basmati rice. It was still roughly twenty-five percent full. There are traces of gravy and juices in the rice, and two wooden chopsticks, also marked 'Bara Miyako.''

Marvia said, 'Hold on.' She jotted a few more words on her pad, then told Kern to resume.

'Okay. The third container is the

winner. Seems that the victim ordered an Oriental seafood stew. I had to call in a consulting marine biologist from the Steinhart Aquarium in the city to identify the specimens, which were coated and partially covered in a thin gravy of water, flour, soya, and natural juices.'

'And the ingredients were — ?'

Laura Kern took a deep breath. '*Hapolochlaena maculosa*, *Arothron meleagris*, and *Gonyaulax catanella*.'

'Spell, please.'

Kern spelled.

'And now, in English.'

'Okay, Sergeant. First, *Hapolochlaena* is the Australian blue-ringed octopus. Small, innocuous-looking creature with a gentle disposition. But its poison can be absorbed through the skin, even the back of the hand, and even a small dose can be fatal. It attacks the central nervous system, causing paralysis, including cessation of breathing and heart function. It's chemically unique, but its effect is similar to that of the venom of the genus *Naja*, the best known member being the Egyptian cobra.'

Marvia whistled. 'What about the others?'

'*Arothron* is the common pufferfish. They come in various sizes, and may be kept as aquarium fish. In some cultures, notably Japanese haute cuisine, the meat of *Arothron* is highly prized. But it must be cleaned with extreme care because its ovaries and guts secrete an extremely toxic substance. Grilled pufferfish, or *fugu*, is regarded as a supreme delicacy; but even with the greatest of care, there are several fatalities each year, almost always in Asia, from consuming *fugu*.'

'Right. And the last one?'

'*Gonyaulax* is a family of microorganisms called dinoflagellates. They thrive as parasites in many bivalves such as oysters and mussels, but no bivalve meat or shells were found in the specimen.'

'Suppose they were cooked and shelled, then only the meat was served?'

'Subject might have consumed the bivalve meat. He would have consumed his share of *Gonyaulax*, and there would be traces left in the sauce in the container. Absolutely.'

133

'Poisonous, right?'

'Oh, highly. On the standard toxicity rating scale of one to six, blue-ringed octopus, *fugu*, and *Gonyaulax* are all sixes. Anybody who consumed any of the three would have a good chance at a quick death.'

'How quick? If the subject smoked part of that joint and then ate as much food as would have been missing from those containers, how long would he have remained conscious? And how long would he have stayed alive?'

'*Fugu* poisoning would start pretty quickly, causing death within a matter of hours. *Gonyaulax* might be a little slower. *Hapolochlaena* is usually absorbed through the epidermis — first effects within minutes, death within twenty-four hours. I don't know of anybody actually ingesting it before, but I'd guess that the toxin would start to enter the bloodstream through the tongue and go right on through the esophagus and stomach lining. That would probably be the quickest. That would be the one that killed the subject. All the chemicals inhaled from that joint — I don't know, they would really complicate the equation. But I'd say, if he sat down to smoke a little dope before dinner and then started eating that seafood stew, he'd never make it through the meal. Unconscious in five minutes, dead in ten, would be my guess.'

'Thanks, Laura. How soon can you get me the complete report, in writing?'

'Couple of days, Sergeant.'

'Good . . . Oh, that matchbook. Was there anything odd about it?'

'Six matches removed, only four in the ashtray. But he could have been carrying the matchbook around for days.'

Marvia thanked her and hung up. She recalled that the matchbook was from the Club San Remo, an old establishment on University Avenue. The building had started as an upscale nightclub catering to young professionals, then fallen on hard times. It had operated under a series of names and owners until it was taken over by Solomon San Remo, a shady character best known for running a series of charity scams. As the Club San Remo, the place became a punk music club. It was also a notorious drug hangout, and had finally given up the ghost when a punk musician died of a poisoned drug dose in the middle of a performance. That was the end. Solomon San Remo wound up in prison, and his club had been razed to make room for a low-cost housing block.

Bob Bjorner, Radio Red, dying with a couple of drug-cocktail cigarettes in his ashtray and a murderous array of poisonous sea-dwellers in his belly, and a Club San Remo matchbook in his possession? Very peculiar. And before Bjorner's body was turned over to the coroner's technicians, his pockets had been checked, and there was no bag of cannabis buds or any other drug paraphernalia there. He might have carried the slim joints into the studio with him.

What about the ashtray itself? That wouldn't have gone off to Laura Kern; that would be right here in the evidence room. Marvia went there, checked out the Bjorner materials, and carried the ashtray back to her desk.

It was ordinary enough: round, heavy,

dark-gray smoked glass, smudged with ash. The ash smudge only partially blocked the image painted in the center: a circular logo of three nude females, one curved in a letter C, one as an S, and the third contorted into an R, her upper torso and arms forming the top loop and her legs arranged to make the lower inverted V. CSR. Club San Remo. Marvia returned the ashtray to the evidence room.

The Club San Remo was out of business — even the building was gone, but Marvia knew where Solomon San Remo was. Where she had helped to put him — in San Quentin Prison. It was not too late to visit Solomon San Remo today. But first she grabbed a petition for a search warrant. If Bjorner had died of poisoned food from Bara Miyako, she wanted to get a thorough report on everything in the place — kitchen, storerooms, garbage. The technicians would do a good job of that, and if there remained any trace of the poisoned food, that would be seized as evidence.

It seemed like a good lead, but it was

one of those proverbial, too-good-to-be-true clues. If you planned a poisoning, you wouldn't order toxic food from a restaurant and have them deliver it in containers with their logo, address, and phone number neatly printed on the side. Unless somebody at the restaurant was the killer. Or unless a third party had a reason to kill the victim, and knew a lot about toxic marine life, and had the opportunity to tamper with the order between the time it left the restaurant and the time it reached Studio B. And, and, and . . .

She had plenty of other things to do, including reading the canvass reports on the businesses surrounding KRED. And there would be follow-up interviews that she would want to handle personally. Still, San Quentin was not that long a trip — and she wanted to get Saintly Solly's input.

She picked up the phone, called the prison, and got through to a deputy warden who walked her through the drill she already knew. In a nutshell, Solomon San Remo was doing his time, and he

138

didn't have to talk to Sergeant Plum if he didn't want to. Even though he was a convicted felon, he still had his Miranda rights, and he could demand a lawyer during their meeting.

The deputy warden went off and checked with Solly, then came back and told Marvia that Mr. San Remo would be delighted to chat with her today at a mutually convenient time and place. They settled on an interrogation room at Q.

*　*　*

Marvia's car pulled up to the guard station at San Quentin. The guard knew she was coming and waved her through. She turned over her S&W automatic at the gate. A tan-uniformed correctional officer escorted her to an interrogation room. When she arrived there, Solomon San Remo was waiting. He hadn't lost any weight on prison food, but his complexion now showed a prison pallor. He was alone. He hadn't requested a lawyer. Marvia walked into the interrogation room and heard the bolt ride into place behind her.

San Remo wore standard prison issue, a denim shirt and jeans. He said, 'Sergeant Plum.'

'Mr. San Remo.' They didn't shake hands.

'What can I do for you, Sergeant?'

'Have you heard about the death of Robert Bjorner?'

'Radio Red? Sure. We try and keep up, despite everything.'

'Huh. And how's your life these days?'

'Well, the fellas seem to think I ratted out my friends to get a break on my sentence. So I keep pretty much to myself.'

'They have you in protective segregation.'

'Right. So I watch TV, do a little exercise, read a lot. Not too bad. I've been catching up on the books I always meant to get to and never did.'

'Look, I want to know about Bob Bjorner. Your connection with him.' San Remo's face was a picture of innocence. 'Why did you agree to see me, Solly?'

'To relieve the boredom.'

'You don't have a parole hearing coming up, do you? What are your plans, if they let you out?'

San Remo dropped his bland expression. 'They wouldn't put me on the Witness Protection Program.'

'I guess what you had to offer wasn't good enough. Let's see ... I think you ratted out your own brother, didn't you?'

'He was a goner anyhow. How dumb can you get? Selling speedballs and sharing needles with his own customers.'

'And you gave us a couple of other chumps, but nobody big. Just one really big guy would have made a lot of difference.'

The light of panic appeared in San Remo's eyes. 'You know if I did that I'd be a dead man.'

'But you might have got WPP.'

'Couldn't risk it. I'll serve my time and I'll walk out of this joint and disappear into the woodwork. Grow a mustache, change my name, move away.'

'Right. But you need the parole first, don't you? Then you can do the rest of it.'

'That's right. So what do you want, Sergeant? What's this about Radio Red? I heard that Bjorner died in the broadcast studio. I listen to KRED on earphones sometimes. They've been carrying on like somebody shot the pope, but I think I detect a slightly false note in all the grief. Am I right, or am I right?'

'I think a few of the tears being shed are crocodile tears.'

'So where do I come in?'

'You're sure you never knew Bjorner?'

'Sergeant Plum.' He leaned forward. 'I don't love you, I don't love cops, but I want my parole and I want to score points, you get it? So believe me, if I could tell you anything about Bjorner, I would. I never met the man.'

Marvia decided to play her cards. 'When Bjorner died, there was an ashtray on the table with a matchbook in it. The matchbook said Club San Remo. The ashtray had an enameled logo painted in the bottom. And what do you think the logo was?'

'Club San Remo. You like the logo? Those willowy figures? You know the studio actually hired models to drape themselves into those shapes?'

Marvia waited for him to continue.

'Club's been gone since that blasted raid you pulled on us. And I'm in this joint. So I don't know where Radio Red got my ashtray.'

Marvia played her last card. 'Bjorner was smoking a fancy drug cocktail when he died. A joint with grass and hash. And a trace of coke and smack.'

San Remo frowned. 'That shouldn't have done him in.'

'I don't think he died of an OD. But I want to know where he got the stuff; who his connection was. And the Club San Remo paraphernalia points straight here. Don't you think, Solly?'

'I swear I never laid eyes on the man.'

'No idea who might have?'

San Remo closed his eyes. Marvia counted silently. 'You ever come across a fellow named Steve Insetta? Old Berkeley hand?'

'Tell me about him,' Marvia said.

'Minor '60s figure; dropped a little too much acid is the story. Got fascinated by bugs. His name *means* bug, you know, in Italian. He used to hang around the club until I barred him for selling drugs on the premises.'

'You're kidding.'

'He was stealing supplies, too. He'd sell some kid a lid of grass and make up a complimentary package with a Club San Remo ashtray, a book of matches, and a roach clip. We had some of those made up — purely as novelties, you understand — and gave them to special customers.'

'Sure you did.'

'Well, we barred Insetta. I'm guessing that he made off with a batch of our ashtrays and so on, and if he was buddies with Bjorner, he must have given him the stuff. That's all, that's my guess, and I want my brownie points.'

Marvia stood up. 'I guess we've gone about as far as we're going, Solly. Good luck. Drop me a line sometime.' She took a few steps to the door and rapped for the guard. Then she turned back and asked another question. 'You said Insetta dropped too much acid. How do you know that? What did he do?'

'He went to a tattoo artist and he got a fancy tattoo on his face. I told you he loved bugs. He got a big blue beetle tattooed on his face. The fool.'

10

Crossing the bridge back to the East Bay, Marvia couldn't help thinking about that logo. Club San Remo. She'd seen it elsewhere and not paid attention. Where had that been? Where?

Solomon San Remo had ordered roach clips made with his club's logo on them. Blue Beetle stole a batch of them and gave them out when he sold dope.

That was it! The roach clip she'd taken away from Jamie and Hakeem. She'd been too angry and too frightened, a mother and not a cop, when she'd found out what the boys were doing, to preserve the evidence. She'd thrown it in a Dumpster, and good riddance. But now she remembered the design of the roach clip. Human forms, intertwined.

Two years after the club had been demolished, Blue Beetle and Acid Alice were still giving away Club San Remo paraphernalia as goodwill presents to their favored clients. Including Marvia's son and his best friend. And including the late Robert Bjorner, Radio Red.

She still didn't have an official cause of death for Bjorner, but considering the leftovers in his food container, there wasn't much doubt about what it would be. That meant that the dope connection, the Blue Beetle connection, didn't have anything to do with Bjorner's death. Or did it? Maybe the 'clean' drugs and the poisoned food were connected in some way.

What the heck did it all mean?

Marvia still needed to follow up on the officers' canvass. She was almost ready to brainstorm this case, and she was convinced now that she did want Dorothy Yamura to sit in on the meeting.

The Blue Beetle connection alone had made the visit to San Quentin worthwhile. Solly would get his brownie points, all right, and he'd get his parole and walk out of prison and start his new life. If somebody didn't shove a shank between his ribs first.

Back at BPD she took one look at her

desk and abandoned the idea of clearing it today. She didn't want to check out another black-and-white, and Barbara Jordan Boulevard was an easy walk from McKinley Avenue. She jammed her uniform cap on her head and started out on foot.

At KRED she found Jessie Loman seated at the receptionist's desk. Jessie looked up at Marvia and blinked owlishly behind her metal-framed oval lenses. 'Uh, hi. Can I . . . ?'

Marvia asked if Ms. Mbolo was in and Jessie Loman confirmed she'd seen her a few minutes ago.

Marvia headed upstairs to her office. The door was open and the room was empty. She heard a voice and found Mbolo on a terrace overlooking a small garden and the backs of a row of low-rise commercial buildings.

Mbolo was sitting at what looked like a lawn table, complete with umbrella. She lowered a glass of iced tea beside a deli sandwich. With her other hand she was clicking away at the keys of a desk calculator, muttering numbers. She had a pencil shoved into her dreadlocks, its yellow shaft bright against the black curls. Dressed in her colorful robes, she looked like an accountant trying to balance the budget of some African republic. She smiled up at Marvia and gestured her to a metal chair.

For the first time, Marvia noticed a small golden Star of David hanging on a fine chain around Mbolo's neck. Mbolo slid her chair away from the table, out of the shade. Her star glittered in the afternoon sunlight.

'I was in the neighborhood and just thought I'd drop in. If you have a few minutes.'

Mbolo's smile widened.

'I want to talk with you about Robert Bjorner.'

'Of course.'

'Have you had any further thoughts, Ms. Mbolo? And, by the way, we ran a check with Sacramento, and that isn't your only name, is it?'

Mbolo lowered her eyes momentarily. 'That is true. I had a different name in Ethiopia. Once I escaped the Dirgue I did not wish to advertise my presence in America, so I changed it.'

'Your name was — ' Marvia caught a look from Mbolo. She opened her notebook and wrote *Tamar Tasira* and showed the page to Mbolo. The woman nodded and held out her hand. Marvia tore the page from her notebook and gave it to her and Sun Mbolo pulled a book of matches from the folds of her African robe and lit one and burned the scrap of paper. Marvia watched her carefully. The matchbook had a design on its cover — three human figures warped into the initials CSR.

'Have you remembered anything more about Mr. Bjorner?' Marvia asked her. 'Any idea who might have wanted to kill him?'

Mbolo shook her head. 'As I told you, Sergeant, there has been a dispute within the staff of KRED between those of us who wish to bring it into the modern era, pay our bills on time, not go crying to our listeners for contributions every few weeks, not rely on government handouts — and those who wish to stop the hands of the clock. Perhaps to turn them back.'

Marvia waited for her to continue.

'I always thought it was odd, you know, Sergeant, that KRED accepted government funding while attacking the government on a daily basis. Then when congress started cutting us back, planning to end our funding, our people were furious. They live on handouts, yet they wish to attack the givers and they become outraged when the givers try to influence the way they — we — spend the money we are given. That is why I wish to get us off the federal dole, much as I disagree with government policies.'

The woman lifted her iced tea. 'I am so sorry. Would you like some? This is my late lunch, I am afraid.'

Marvia declined the offer. 'And of course Bjorner was on the other side of this dispute. Ms. Mbolo, did you know what Bjorner was going to say on his show the day he died?'

'Radio Red? No, I never saw his scripts in advance. We never see scripts in advance at KRED. That is Oceana policy. Always has been. The majority of our broadcasters do not even use scripts. You cannot use scripts for an interview or a call-in show. Even the disc jockeys do most of their work ad-lib. That is the way things are done around here.'

Marvia frowned. 'I thought there was something about forbidden words, FCC investigations and even congressional hearings?'

Mbolo sighed resignedly. 'All the time. But we make sure that our on-air personnel know the station's policies. They know the forbidden words; we hold seminars for them on FCC regulations and on copyright and slander. And of course there are professional ethics and broadcast standards. Other than that, once they are on the air they are on their own.'

Marvia nodded. 'Would you recognize Nikita Khrushchev's speech about Joseph Stalin's crimes?'

'I certainly would. Does the whole world not know that speech?'

'Not really. What would you say if I told you that Robert Bjorner's last Radio Red program was simply the text of Khrushchev's speech?'

'I do not know what I would say. Was it? You took his script, I know.'

'I did, and I had it transcribed from Braille so I could read it. I didn't recognize the text, but I checked with a source and he spotted it at once. He says that people like Bob Bjorner often use that kind of material as code. My source says that Bjorner was using Khrushchev's words to attack you. His condemnation of the so-called cult of personality, the purges, the removal of critics, were all meant to apply to KRED.'

Mbolo nodded. 'Ingenious. Even plausible. But — so what?'

'So, people engaged in disputes sometimes go beyond words.'

'You have concluded that Bjorner was killed?'

'Yes.'

'Are you accusing me?'

'Not at all. I'm just asking you for help.' Marvia leaned toward Mbolo. 'Where did you get that matchbook?'

Mbolo looked startled. When she didn't reply, Marvia said, 'Isn't KRED a non-smoking building?'

'It is. Except here on the terrace. This is considered outside. Some people smoke out here. I do not. I just happened to pick up a matchbook. They — sometimes the starter on my stove does not work right. At home. And I light the burner with a match. So I like to keep matches around.'

'You didn't answer my question. Where did you happen to pick up the matchbook?'

'In the staff lounge. Next to the upstairs rest rooms, we have a little lounge with a gas burner and a fridge. There is a big box of matchbooks there. Somebody must have brought in a whole carton of the things; we have been using them for years. I think they came from some old nightclub over on University that closed down long ago.'

Damn! For a moment it looked as if she was about to tie Mbolo to Bjorner and to Steve Insetta, aka Blue Beetle. Now it looked as if everybody at KRED who used matches would be using Club San Remo matches. Just to make sure, she asked Mbolo to walk her to the lounge and show her the box of matchbooks.

There they were. There must have been a thousand of them when the carton was full, and there were still hundreds. She picked up a few and slipped them into her pocket. They weren't evidence, just information.

Marvia didn't get anything more from Mbolo. She had the feeling that Mbolo knew things that she wasn't telling; that in some way she wanted to say more but was holding back.

Marvia pulled a business card from her wallet. She scribbled on it, then handed it to Mbolo. 'You call me if you get anything more. If you can't reach me at the printed number, you can call me at this other one. They'll patch you through. I want you to be able to reach me anytime. If you feel it's important, I don't care, day or night, call.'

Their hands touched as Mbolo accepted the card. Marvia sensed a tremor in Mbolo's hand and something in her voice when she said, 'Very well, I shall.' But nothing more came.

As Marvia passed the receptionist's desk, Jessie Loman smiled and waved. Marvia smiled back and left the building. She stood in front of the KRED/Oceana building, then turned and entered an adjacent storefront. The display windows were lettered in bright colors: 'Amazon Rain Forest.' Opening the front door caused a bell to ring, but before anyone responded to it, Marvia felt a blast of heat and moisture. For a second she felt as if she'd stepped into an old Carmen Miranda movie, then she shoved the thought out of her mind. It was a Bart Lindsey kind of image, and he was out of her life; she had seen to that.

Ferns and lianas hung from the rafters. Miniature palm trees, their roots in wooden barrels and orchids clinging to their trunks, seemed to fill every available space. A small wooden bridge arched over an artificial stream. She heard a screech, and looked into the glittering black eye of a dark-feathered bird with the biggest beak she'd ever seen.

With a rumble of tires on wood, a woman in a motorized wheelchair came rolling over the bridge. She had close-cropped light brown hair and thick eyebrows over startlingly blue eyes. She was clad in a magenta 'Amazon Rain Forest' T-shirt and faded blue jeans. Her wheelchair was controlled with small movements of two fingers.

She looked up at Marvia and said, 'Welcome to our little shop of pleasures. What can I do for you?'

'I'm Sergeant Plum. Are you the proprietor?'

'Margarita Horowitz.' She nodded in lieu of shaking hands. 'I'm one of them. My partner's in the back tending to some angels with ick.'

'Pardon me?'

'Angelfish. With ichthyophthirius. It's a parasite disease of fresh water fishes. It's treatable, but you have to be careful 'cause it's damned contagious and you can wipe out a whole tank if you don't watch it. But that isn't what you came to see me about, is it?'

'No. I'm investigating the death of Robert Bjorner at KRED two days ago.'

'I already told that cop everything I

157

know. What was his name — Holliman? No, Holloway. Pleasant round-faced young fellow. He wanted to know where I was when Red bit the big one. You his boss, Sarge? You checking up on the rookies?'

'No, we always follow up on canvasses, or try to. And how did you know that Bjorner had bit it?'

Horowitz jerked her head toward the back of the store. 'Come on back, I'll show you. We always listen to Radio Red.' She rolled back over the wooden bridge and through a pair of saloon doors into a brightly lit workroom, Marvia following. A stocky woman wearing an apron over her T-shirt and jeans was transferring a clear liquid from a small brown bottle to a large aquarium tank via eye-dropper.

'Susan, this is Sergeant Plum. Sergeant, my partner, Susan Gerber.'

The stocky woman turned to face Marvia. 'D'ja do. Sorry I'm busy.' She returned to her work.

Margarita Horowitz grinned. 'Susan is the Bay Area's greatest fish doctor. She gets calls from the Steinhart Aquarium, from Pier 39, even from Monterey.' She smiled at her partner, but Susan Gerber was concentrating on the aquarium. 'Look, Sergeant, business is a little slow at the moment. I think we can talk in the store. Would you mind?' Without waiting for a reply, she rolled through the saloon doors and across the wooden bridge.

They were back in the rain forest. A huge red parrot walked to the end of a tree branch and cocked its head at Marvia, then screamed at her.

'Quit it, Michael!' Margarita shook her head. 'Sorry about that. Michael loves shiny things. I think he just told your badge that he's in love with it.' To the big bird she said, 'Back off, goofy. Leave the poor cop alone. Okay, Sergeant, what can I do for the forces of justice in our community?'

'Officer Holloway's report says that you knew Robert Bjorner.' Marvia was taking notes by hand today. The tape recorder was reserved for longer interrogations.

Margarita Horowitz nodded. 'I used to fight with him at staff meetings. Then he held the door for me when I came back. *Tres gallant.*'

'Came back?'

'To KRED. I had a program there before my injury. *An Hour With* . . . Some fun. Now it's *The Other-Abled Hour*. Not as much fun, but it's more important.'

'Tell me about your program, and how Robert Bjorner was involved.'

'KRED never paid me, you know. Still doesn't.'

That fitted with what Marvia had heard from Jessie Loman.

'I started out as a campus activist at Cal.' A wistful smile crossed her face. 'Was that ever fun. We thought burning brassieres was a profound feminist statement. Burning bras and smoking dope — whoops, you gonna bust me for admitting that I used to smoke dope, Sergeant?'

'Please. KRED. Bob Bjorner.'

'Okay. I got my show in 1980. *An Hour with Sojourner Strength*.'

'Not Margarita Horowitz?'

'Not the right pizzazz. Mama named me Naomi Ruth Horowitz. I changed it to Margarita in high school. More exotic. That's what I use now for most things.

Sojourner Strength was my movement name at Cal, and it's been my air name since I got into radio.'

Now we were getting somewhere. 'You started at KRED in 1980? And Bjorner was there already?'

'That's correct. Station was still in the old building over on Spalding. There was only one way in and out of the station, no wheelchair lift or ramp, but I was able-bodied then. Bob was doing his show, *The News and What It Means*. He was a real pioneer. One of the first people to join KRED after the four founders. The news was basically whatever came off the wire, but the wire wasn't AP, it was TASS. And what the news meant was whatever TASS said it meant. Every time the party line zigged, Bob zigged. Every time it zagged, he zagged.'

'And now . . . ?'

'My show now is not *The Disability Hour*. It's *The Other-Abled Hour*. You can do things I can't do and I can do things that you can't do. Try teaching a dinosaur to sing that one. And instead of talking about getting girl sportswriters into boys' locker rooms, I talk about access and nondiscrimination.'

'About Bjorner . . . '

'I knew him at the old station, before I was injured. Then when I was rehabbed enough to get back into broadcasting; they were already in the new building. It's great. I can get in and out on my own, and I'm back on the air. When I came back to KRED, Bob Bjorner was still doing his show. Different name, *World News Analysis*, but it was the same ideological guff. They never did know what to do with him. I mean, after Khrushchev's boffo speech, poor Bob went into a complete funk. Joe Stalin was his number-one hero. Now he was a bad guy. But Bob hung in there. Did I tell you he could still see medium-well when we were in the old building? His eyes only got really bad — I mean, *really* bad — the past few years.'

'When did you last see Bob Bjorner?'

'Well, Susan and I opened Amazon Rain Forest two years ago. We got a lot of publicity at first, then business got very slow, and now it's building steadily. We'll be in the black pretty soon. Bob used to come in once in a while; his brother would drop him early at KRED and he'd come in here instead and hang out before his show.'

'Was he here on Monday — the day he died?'

'Let's see, I think — '

'No, he wasn't!' Susan Gerber called from the back room.

Horowitz looked puzzled. 'I thought he was. Huh, I guess not, then. Maybe I was thinking of last Monday. You know, he came in a lot. I thought he was here this week, though, but maybe I was mistaken.'

'What did he do while he was here?'

'Well, he came in and chatted a little. He was really pissed at Sun Mbolo and the whole way the station's going. He thought they were turning it into a bland middle-of-the-road operation. Mbolo and her crowd were giving up the fight, abandoning the cause, becoming capitalists.'

'How do you feel about that?'

'Do I look like I give a damn? I don't care about that Karl Marx crap; never did. I care about real stuff.'

'Did you tell that to Bjorner?'

'Hell, Sarge, I fought with Radio Red for years on end. I think the old coot had a crush on me. When his partner died — you knew about Anitra Colón, his life partner, didn't you? — when she died, I didn't think Bob was going to navigate. I used to go and cook for him, take care of him. If we'd been the same age I think he would have asked me to move in with him. I kind of loved the old buzzard myself. But we fought like wildcats.'

Marvia said, 'All the people at the station who were involved in this battle over broadcast policy — how high did their passions rise? Was there anybody who had a personal grudge against Bjorner? Anyone you'd describe as an enemy?'

Horowitz shook her head. 'Nobody.'

'Was Bjorner carrying anything with him the last time you saw him?'

'His lunch. He always ate his lunch in the studio before he went on the air. He'd lock himself in so nobody could get at him, and toke up a little, and then eat a late lunch. I know Jem Waller used to have fits. Strictly against the rules, and Jem was chief engineer for years. Anybody else, he would have had a showdown, and if they refused to toe the line they would have been out of KRED. But Radio Red was such an institution, Jem couldn't touch him. Every so often they'd have a big blow-up; and Jem always got his way, officially, but Bob just ignored him and kept bringing his stash and his lunch into the station.'

'Do you know what Bob had for lunch the day he died?'

'He always carried brown paper bags that said Bara Miyako on them. Susan and I eat there ourselves, once in a while. Used to be pretty good, then they seemed to slack off for a while, then they got a new chef and changed their menu some, and it's first-rate now. Bob was such a conservative guy, he stuck with Bara Miyako through thick and thin.'

'Do you know the couple who run Bara Miyako?'

'Mr. and Mrs. Fuji. I don't know their first names. Nice old couple. Very traditional, too. Maybe that's why Bob liked their place so much.'

Marvia turned a page in her notebook. 'That's my next stop. I'll say hello there, for you.' She'd supervised a search of the restaurant — for once the judge hadn't given her a hard time about issuing the warrant she'd requested. Now it was follow-up time. She closed the notebook and slipped it into her pocket.

'Ms. Horowitz, you said that you know the people at Bara Miyako. How's their English?'

Horowitz smiled. 'It's just fine. Better than mine, I think.'

'Thank you, Ms. Horowitz. If you think of anything else . . . ' She held a card toward the other woman, then followed the gesture she made with her chin and slipped the card into her shirt pocket.

11

Stepping out of Amazon Rain Forest onto the sidewalk, Marvia shivered. The streetlamps had blinked on and darkness was encroaching. The fog had crept inland from the bay, and the sky had turned a somber gray.

She stood outside Bara Miyako, studying the red rose logo painted inside the glass and scanning the diners beyond. The restaurant was decorated in pale grays and paler yellows, with only an occasional red rose to liven the decor. There were white tablecloths and better-dressed early diners than Marvia would have expected on this part of Barbara Jordan Boulevard.

Marvia stepped inside. A young Japanese woman wearing a cloth headband and Bara Miyako apron scurried to greet her. She hadn't been at the restaurant when Marvia was there with the technicians. She looked worried. Marvia asked for a table. She hadn't eaten since her breakfast with Jamie; it was hard to believe that had been just this morning.

She sat down and the young woman offered her a menu. She placed her order.

After finishing the meal, she washed it down with green tea, wishing she could have ordered a jug of sake instead. But she was on duty. When she paid her check, the elderly Japanese woman who took her money was Mrs. Fuji.

Marvia said, 'How are you, Mrs. Fuji? I'm happy to see you again.'

The small woman looked frightened. She wore her gray hair in a bun with a pair of decorative rods through it. She nodded and whispered, 'Yes.'

'Could I speak with you, please? And is Mr. Fuji here?'

Again, the whispered yes.

Mr. Fuji wore a dark blue suit and white shirt. He was barely taller than his wife, and looked to be the same age — early seventies. He had been in the kitchen supervising the chef, and returned to the dining room and spoke briefly with the young woman before

168

leading Marvia to the restaurant's small office.

He ushered Marvia inside. She had to remind him to include his wife. A desk filled most of the room and a filing cabinet stood in the corner. A framed copy of the Bara Miyako menu hung on the wall behind the desk. There were only two chairs in the room, and Mrs. Fuji brought another from the dining room.

No one sat down until introductions and business cards were exchanged. It was as if their previous meeting had never happened. Mrs. Fuji sat beside the desk, her hands in her lap, her head lowered. Mr. Fuji sat behind the desk, opposite Marvia.

'I'm investigating the death of Mr. Bjorner at KRED two days ago.'

Mr. Fuji said, 'You were here before. Did we not assist you at that time?'

'I appreciate that. We have to search for evidence.'

'Were the results not satisfactory?'

Marvia let her breath out. 'I just have some questions, if you don't mind helping . . . Can you tell me where you were when

Mr. Bjorner died?'

The old couple exchanged glances. They must have been in their restaurant, of course. It was a lot of work to run a restaurant. They were not wealthy people. They had built Bara Miyako from nothing and made it a success, but they both still worked many hours a day. But then, when exactly did Mr. Bjorner die?

Marvia told them. Mr. Fuji said, 'I was working in the office and my wife was supervising our chef, Mr. Kojima.'

Marvia indicated the framed menu. 'Do you ever serve pufferfish in your restaurant?'

The Fujis drew back in their chairs. 'You need a special certificate to prepare *fugu*.'

'Yes. And — ?'

Mr. Fuji said, 'No, never. Our new chef, Mr. Kojima, is the finest we could find. But even he does not have the certificate needed to prepare *fugu*. And we cannot buy puffer from our suppliers. It only lives in the western ocean. We use fresh fish only, from the Okutaro Hanto

Market on San Pablo. You know it, north of University?'

Marvia made a note. The search had turned up no sign of pufferfish, but in a restaurant the simplest way to destroy the remnants of a toxic dish is simply to toss them into a charcoal fire.

'How long have you been in business?'

'Twenty-two years here. Before that, in Oakland, on the Embarcadero.'

'Did you know Robert Bjorner?'

Mrs. Fuji smiled. 'He was a good customer. Once, sometimes twice a week. Every Monday, sometimes other days too. He liked our food. A very nice man, very good customer.'

Mr. Fuji said, 'Mr. Bjorner's death was a tragedy.'

'Did he eat here in your restaurant, or take food out?'

'Sometimes here, sometimes out.'

'Was he here this Monday?'

'No!' Mr. Fuji got in his answer before his wife could speak.

'Do you keep records of your sales? Order slips, credit card slips?'

'Everything.'

'Do you remember if Mr. Bjorner used a credit card?'

Mr. Fuji shook his head. 'Never. Always paid cash.'

'And you're sure he wasn't in this week?'

'We are certain.'

I'll just bet you are. 'How many people work in your restaurant?'

Mr. Fuji sighed. 'We are very poor people. Just my wife and myself, chef and waitress, and one cleanup boy. Korean boy, Bo Kim. That's all.'

That jibed with the report she'd got from the patrol officer who had done the canvass. She looked at her notebook. Hiroshi Kojima, Yaeko Kato, Bo Kim. 'Do you know where they were Monday afternoon?'

'All at work. Everybody here works very hard.'

Marvia closed her notebook and thanked the Fujis. She asked if she might speak with Mr. Kojima and Ms. Kato and Mr. Kim. Mr. Fuji was very upset at that. It was the beginning of the dinner hour and the restaurant would soon be at its busiest. They were poor people and had to work very hard to make a living. Their work could not be interrupted. And Chef Kojima and Ms. Kato and Mr. Kim also had Miranda rights, did they not? Marvia conceded that they did. Even if they weren't suspects, they could just tell her that they were busy and they didn't want to talk to her. Mr. Fuji assured her that his employees would choose to exercise their rights. If she insisted on questioning them, they would decline to speak with her. She thanked them for their cooperation and left.

Marvia checked out Beiderbecke's Wax Cylinder, but it was closed for the day. Well, it was getting late anyhow. She hurried back to McKinley Avenue and showered and changed to civvies and drove home.

Gloria had eaten. She muted the TV and dropped the cordless phone to her lap. Without taking her eyes from the image on the TV, she said, 'Call Mr. White. He's very upset.' She held the telephone vaguely in Marvia's direction.

Marvia shook her head; she'd use her

own phone for this one. Besides, before dialing Hakeem's dad, she wanted to talk with Jamie.

She discovered that he wasn't in the house. She peered into the backyard, then closed the kitchen door softly and padded across the scruffy lawn to the old blue oak and climbed to the tree-house.

Jamie sat on the wooden planking and watched Marvia climb into the tree-house. He was wearing his headphones. He didn't offer any assistance, but he didn't try to stop her either. When she got inside, she sat down cross-legged, facing him the way she had sat facing her brother three decades before.

Jamie slipped the headphones from his ears and set them on the plank floor. 'Mom.'

'Hello, Jamie.' She held out her hand, palm forward, and he placed his against hers. His hands were as big as hers now. He was already as tall as Marvia.

'Hakeem is grounded,' Jamie said. 'Forever. His people are Muslims, Mom. They're really strict with him. He did what you told him; he told me in school

174

today. I think his dad was madder about drinking brew than about smoking weed. They'll never let him out again. Straight to school and straight home after. And they took out his TV and his box, and they made him wipe the games off his disc. They said they knew he could download more, but they'd cut off his hand if he did. They do that, you know.'

'I'm glad you told me, Jamie. They phoned here and your grandma took the call.'

'Yeah?'

'Yes. I'm supposed to call them back. What would you like me to tell them?'

'Tell them that I bought the stuff from Blue Beetle and Alice. Tell them it wasn't Hakeem's fault.'

'I think it would be best if you'd do that, Jamie. I don't think it would do much good for me to tell them.'

He started to answer, then stopped. He stuck his chin out. She'd known that gesture since he was in diapers — it meant that he was shifting gears. 'It was only a little weed. Mom, you don't know what the kids do at BenBan. You're old and you just don't know what they're doing. Smoking a number is nothing. It's nothing.'

Now she had to stand up to the boy. 'When you're grown up, you'll make your own decisions, Jamie. Right now you are a child, and you are in my custody, and you will do as I tell you. Do you understand that?'

He turned up his face and she saw that it was wet. He whispered, 'I understand you.'

She felt her heart bump and reached out and hugged him before he could pull away. 'You remember Inspector Stillman? He's running the Narcotics Division, and I told him I had an informant.'

'Mom!'

'An anonymous informant. If you help us out, you'll be a hero. I don't want you to do anything dangerous, and I won't let Stillman even ask you to. Will you help us out?'

'Will it get rid of Beetle and Alice?'

'I hope so. But I thought you liked them.'

'I did. Me and Hack. Lots of kids.'

'What changed?'

'You know Tanya Johnson's dead?'

'I heard. I'll go to her funeral on Sunday. I know her parents.'

'Yeah, Mom. You know what she died of?'

'She was visiting her family down south. I didn't even know she was sick, until I heard she'd died.'

'Yeah, well TJ was a cool person; I really liked her . . . She died of AIDS.'

'I didn't know.'

'She was shooting meth.'

'I didn't know.' Marvia heard a roaring in her ears. She didn't know anything. Cop Marvia and Mom Marvia glared at each other in bafflement and rage.

'She was working for Beetle and Alice. She was their cutout. They gave her free stuff for it. She got AIDS from a needle.'

Marvia felt numb. She had to get off by herself and get calm, but right now she couldn't do that. 'All right. For now, let's go back to the house. You're going to call Hakeem's parents and tell them what you told me.' She had already backed through the opening of the tree-house and set her feet on a two-by-four. She looked up and saw Jamie above her. He held out his hand and she took it and steadied herself.

On the ground, she put her arm around her son's shoulders. 'Jamie, is it true? That you bought everything and gave it to Hakeem?'

'Mom, you know what you always tell me about being a cop?'

'What?'

'Everybody always lies to cops.'

12

Jamie Wilkerson said, 'They want you to come over now. I talked to Hack's dad and he said he'd rather see you in person. Do you want to come over to their house, or should they come here?'

For the moment they were insulated from Gloria; Jamie had called Hakeem's parents from Marvia's telephone while Marvia remained in the hallway.

'All right. Tell him I'll be right over.'

Jamie passed on her message, then hung up. Marvia led the way to the kitchen, where she faced Jamie again. 'You didn't want me to listen while you talked; I respected that. But now I want you to tell me about it.'

'I told Hack's dad that I bought the dope and invited Hakeem over to play Nintendo and he didn't know anything about it.'

'Did Mr. White believe you?'

Jamie shrugged. 'I guess he did.'

'All right. And you agree that I'll talk to Inspector Stillman about this.'

'Mom, it was just a little weed.'

They were back to that. She invited him to sit down with her. 'Listen, Jamie, I wish I could spend more time with you. I'll try. And I'll try and get Tyrone to come around more. I know you like him, and it's good for you to have a man around you. Living with two women can't be too great for a boy your age.'

He nodded. She knew he was waiting for her to get to the point.

'Look, Jamie, we can't all be rap artists or millionaire ballplayers, but we can still have good lives.'

He was still waiting.

'And you see the gangsters — you know they're all going to wind up dead or in prison. You saw the jail where I work.'

'Yeah.'

'That's a *nice* place compared to the serious prisons in this state. You know the rate of crime inside our prisons? You know the rate of AIDS in there?'

He didn't answer.

'Jamie, people don't go from good guy

to creep in one step. They take a little step, and another little step, and another little step. They smoke a little weed, then they snort a little coke, then they shoot a little smack. They carry a knife to school, then they get a little gun. Step by step, Jamie. Until they wind up crackheads or gang-bangers.' She let out her breath. 'All right, Jamie.' She stood up. 'Will Hakeem's parents let him play baseball?'

'I don't know.'

'I'll ask them.'

* * *

Yasmina White answered the doorbell and Marvia stepped inside the brown shingle house. It was less than a full city block from her own home, but Marvia walked past the Johnson house en route. A black wreath hung from the front door.

Jamie Wilkerson and Hakeem White had been playmates since they shared a playpen; they had been in and out of each other's homes for their whole lives. Hakeem had two older sisters. They were nowhere in evidence. Neither was Hakeem.

Marvia followed Yasmina into the living room. Ibrahim White stood up and nodded. '*Assalaam-alaikum*,' he said.

'*Wa-alaikum-salaam.*'

'In the name of God the merciful, the compassionate.' He dipped his head and raised it again. 'Won't you make yourself at home?'

Marvia lowered herself gingerly onto the cushion of a geometrically patterned overstuffed easy chair.

'Mrs. Wilkerson, my boy told me a story yesterday, and I just heard a very different one from your son,' Ibrahim White said. 'Perhaps you can clarify this situation for me.'

'Maybe you'll tell me what they said.'

'Hakeem told me that he bought some marijuana at school and brought it to Jamie's house and you caught them using it. My boy tried to take all the blame on himself. Now just tonight, Jamie told me that *he* was the guilty party and Hakeem the innocent one.'

Yasmina White had left them alone

when Marvia arrived. Now she returned from the kitchen with a tray, a teapot and cups. She poured for her husband and for Marvia, then took a cup for herself and sat on another chair.

Ibrahim lifted his cup, waited for his wife and his guest to do the same, and sipped. Then he lowered the cup and said, 'What do you make of that, Mrs. Wilkerson? Which boy is the criminal?'

'Neither.'

Ibrahim looked startled. 'You'll explain that for me, I hope. They both confessed.'

'Crooks never take the blame. Believe me, I've talked to hundreds of them. Mostly they deny their crimes. And even when they admit they did the deed, it's never their fault. Never. He beat up his wife because she provoked him. He robbed the store because the grocer was cheating him. He sold the crack because the CIA made him do it. He strangled the hooker because she laughed at his little pecker. It's *never* the crook's fault.'

Ibrahim looked shocked. Out of the corner of her eye Marvia saw Yasmina suppress a grin. Finally Ibrahim nodded but did not speak.

'These boys both took the blame,' Marvia said. 'They're good kids. They made a mistake. I think they need a lesson, but I don't think it should be too severe.'

'What do you have in mind, Mrs. Wilkerson?'

'Both boys are grounded.'

'I'm glad to hear that. Hakeem is, of course.'

'Yes. But Jamie told me you'd grounded Hakeem forever. Isn't that a little bit excessive?'

Ibrahim gave an amused snort. 'He is grounded indefinitely. Perhaps he interpreted that as forever. It's all right if he did. We take this very seriously, Mrs. Wilkerson. Hakeem has committed a very serious offense, not merely against the state but against the Almighty. Whether he led your son, or whether he was led by your son, he must bear responsibility for his actions.'

Marvia said, 'I just think that we'll drive these two boys away from us and onto that devil's path if we're too harsh. I think they've learned their lesson. I don't say we can ignore this, but I think we can do more for them with some firm guidance than with harsh punishment.'

'What do you suggest?'

'I think — well, Hakeem is your son, of course. I was going to suggest a week of total grounding, and then next week they could try out for the baseball team. Straight to school, baseball practice, and straight home afterwards.'

Ibrahim furrowed his brow. Marvia watched him as he turned toward his wife. Something passed between them, she knew, but she did not try to read the message.

At last Ibrahim nodded. 'One week total grounding. Then baseball only permitted. Afterwards, homework and prayers. Many, many prayers, and study of the blessed Koran. No hanging out. No skating. No movies. No watching television.'

'Agreed.' Marvia stood up. 'One thing more, Mr. White.'

He raised his eyebrows and waited for the question.

'How would you feel about Hakeem speaking with someone at police headquarters about this situation? I want to get the dealers, not the kids. They're victims. I want to get the people who are selling to them. Would Hakeem give the police a statement?'

'I will see to that.' He stood up and again they exchanged blessings.

Marvia walked home. She'd said nothing of Inspector Stillman to the Whites, or of her conversation with Jamie about Blue Beetle and Acid Alice. But Cop Marvia had emerged at the end of the conversation, and it looked as if she'd got a pledge from Hakeem's father that could prove highly useful. She'd have to do the same with Jamie.

She got home and found a message on the answering machine in her room: 'Call Sun Mbolo.' There was a telephone number.

She picked up the telephone and punched in Sun Mbolo's number, but got an answering machine. She left word that she'd returned the call and would try again in the morning, at KRED.

Minutes later she crawled into bed and clicked on the radio, then turned off the light and closed her eyes. The pillow felt like a soft, welcoming bosom.

The voice of Margarita Horowitz came from the radio. No, she was Sojourner Strength now. That was her broadcast persona. She was talking about Robert Bjorner.

Bob was Radio Red, sisters. Sisters and brothers. He was one of KRED's other-abled heroes. Loss of his vision didn't stop this fighter for justice from carrying on the people's struggle. Nothing could stop Red from carrying on except death itself. And you know, sisters, sisters and brothers, I have a funny feeling.

I want you to share this with me. Share this with your sister, Sojourner Strength. If you're at home in bed, or sitting in your easy chair, turn off all the lights. Well, leave a candle burning if you wish. Yes, light a candle, just one candle. And sit back or lie back and let your eyelids slide down, let them slide down. Not all the way though, not all the way.

Watch the candle's flame flicker. Watch it dance.

That's Radio Red, sisters and brothers.

Bob Bjorner was the heart and soul of KRED. The heart and soul. The heart has ceased to beat but you know the soul lives on, brothers and sisters. The soul lives on.

Sojourner Strength's voice was soothing, insinuating. It seemed as if she were speaking inside Marvia's head. She drifted into sleep.

The rustle of serpents sliding through jungle foliage. The purling of an icy stream as it tumbled down from its mountain headwaters. The screech of brightly colored birds. The sound of soft shoes padding over matted tropical grasses.

'My princess!'

'Hush, Nicholas Train. None must know that I am the Princess. I am simply your companion, Tina Carter, for now.'

The snick of metal on metal and a soft sound, whump! Like a small object striking wood.

'Stay down, Princess Tina! Someone is

firing a gas gun at us!'

'But who could it be? No one even knows we're here in Oaxaca.'

'The army knows. But I trust Colonel Walters, and he assured me that his staff are completely trustworthy.'

Another soft whump!

'Come on, Tina. We're sitting ducks if we stay any longer in the lean-to. We have to get out of here!'

'But where can we go?'

'Into the jungle if we must. I'd rather face the wild beasts than stay here and let our enemy pick us off. Look! The thatch is starting to smolder.'

'They're shooting incendiary rounds at us!'

A creak, the scuttling of two pairs of feet, one shod in heavy boots, the other in light jungle slippers. The eerie, almost supernatural call of a hunting jaguar. A soft crash and the scream of a tropical bird.

'Made it!' Panting.

'Look back — it's a woman!'

'Why — I know her! That's Elsie Desmond. She works for the Parker

Aircraft Company. She was one of the engineers' assistants on the Electro Super Bomber design team.'

'What could she be doing here?'

Another female voice. 'Come out! I know you're hiding in the bushes, Nick Train!'

'She must have learned back at the factory in Arizona. She was always hanging around Wright. How does she know you're here, Nick?'

'She must have learned back at the factory in Arizona. She was always hanging around Wright Martin, Parker's chief test pilot. He's supposed to arrive today, in the Super Bomber.'

'The Super Bomber — here?'

'Yes. Colonel Walters ordered the tests moved here to Oaxaca because this would be the most secure location, safe from Adolf Hitler's saboteurs. Martin is flying the Super Bomber down from Arizona. There's even an observer on board, one of our brave Russian allies, Vladimir Borofsky.'

Marvia stirred. The radio was still on, and without opening her eyes she fumbled for the switch before drifting off again.

★ ★ ★

Marvia woke to the odor of freshly brewed coffee and climbed out of bed. She'd managed to crawl out of her clothes and pull on a set of sweats in lieu of pajamas. Her head was full of strange images and half-remembered words.

She found Jamie in the kitchen eating a bowl of cereal. He said, 'Uncle Ty was here last night while you were at Hack's. I told him you were gonna be right back. He hung out with Gloria watching one of those stupid TV shows, then he said he had to leave. He said he'd try you again. I don't know when. Maybe tonight.'

'Did you and Tyrone talk?'

'Sure.'

'Want to tell me what about?'

'Well, Hack and me and stuff. Baseball.'

'And Beetle and Alice?'

'He's known them for a long time. Said

they're bad news. He says I shouldn't mess with 'em.'

On to the next item. 'I had quite a talk with Hakeem's parents last night, Jamie. We're going to treat you and Hakeem exactly the same. Complete grounding for a week.' He started to protest but she cut him off. 'Then you can try out for the baseball team. That's all. Nothing else. School, baseball practice, home. And no TV, no music, just studying.'

He frowned into his cereal bowl. 'What about your pal the narc?'

'Mr. White says that Hakeem will give a statement to Inspector Stillman. Two will be a lot better than one. Are you still willing to see him, Jamie?'

'Yeah, I guess so.'

'All right.' Marvia poured herself a cup of coffee, opened the refrigerator and took a glass of juice, then sat down opposite Jamie. 'Why are you so willing to go after Beetle and Alice? I thought they were your friends.'

'They sold some kids some smack, and they gave 'em needles and they got AIDS. Berkeley High kids. And they turned a girl I know into a toss-up. She was in a couple of my classes.'

Marvia felt an ice-cold hand grab her insides. 'Who?'

'Don't you remember K'neesha Baldwin?'

'Sure. But the Baldwins moved to Vancouver.'

'Yeah. They got her back, and they have cousins there or something, so they just went.'

Marvia felt a sinking feeling. The cops didn't know as much as a school boy. How much did Mack Stillman know about this? Or Ed Florio at Benjamin Banneker Junior High? Tanya Johnson dead, and K'neesha Baldwin a toss-up whose parents had to leave town with her to get her off crack. Marvia's pulse pounded in her ears. 'Why didn't you tell me this last night, Jamie? Why did you only tell me half of it?'

'I don't know, Mom. I guess I just slept on it.' He looked around, frightened. 'I kept waking up and thinking about it . . . '

Marvia held him by the shoulders. She

saw that he was trying very hard not to cry. 'Just school and straight home, Jamie,' she had to remind him. 'I'll try to get home for dinner, but if I don't that's no excuse. You eat with your grandma if she'll come to the table. Otherwise, you spend the evening with your books.'

13

Marvia parked the black-and-white at the side entrance of KRED and walked around to the front door. She stopped at the receptionist's desk to ask a few questions. 'Does the name Nicholas Train mean anything to you?'

Jessie Loman looked puzzled.

'Tina Carter? Oaxaca?' Marvia persisted. 'Something about a bomber.'

Loman squinted up through her metal-rimmed glasses. 'That's starting to sound familiar. Wait a minute.' She flipped the pages of the KRED program guide, then swung it around and shoved it at Marvia. '*Lon Dayton's OTR Heaven*. Lon's been running a serial lately. I listened to a couple of installments. *Nick Train: Spy-Hunter*. They ran that during the Second World War. Kind of silly, like kid stuff, but kind of fun. Did you stay up and listen last night, Sergeant?'

'Not exactly.' Marvia glanced through

the program guide. 'All right if I keep this?'

'Sure, take it.'

'But I really came in to see Ms. Mbolo this morning.'

Loman shook her head. 'Not in yet. In fact . . . ' She consulted an appointment book, then swung it around for Marvia to see, as she had the program guide. 'You see, there's a funding council meeting today in the city. I don't think she'll be in until tomorrow.'

'And she's in San Francisco for the day, is that right?'

'Yep.'

'Okay, if she happens to call in during the day, would you tell her that I came by to see her? Ask her to phone me, and if we don't connect I'll try and get in touch tonight.'

As long as she was on BJB, she might as well continue checking out the patrol officers' canvass reports. As she was leaving the station she met the ragged woman she'd seen on the night of Robert Bjorner's murder. That time, the woman had walked past Marvia and Herbert

Bjorner. Now she was striding into KRED as if she knew what she was doing. Marvia stopped the woman and asked if she could speak with her for a minute. She showed her badge.

The ragged woman grinned. She looked clean enough, and she had pretty good teeth. She didn't have the blank look of an alcoholic bag lady or the wild eyes of a dangerous schizophrenic. Reaching into a pocket, she fished out a press card with her photo on it beside an oversized KRED logo. 'We're even,' she said. 'What can I do for you, sis?'

Marvia raced to reassess this woman. The name on the badge was Maude Markham. A familiar name; why did she know it? Yes! The San Francisco *Mirror* story on the Bjorner killing. That was what the ragged woman was doing on BJB on Monday night — she was covering the story for the *Mirror*. She must even have had a camera tucked somewhere in her rags. Marvia should have caught that, but she was too busy dealing with Herb Bjorner. But then, why did Markham's press card say KRED?

Marvia said, 'I'm investigating the death of Robert Bjorner.' She offered Markham a business card, and Markham accepted it.

'You're not about to go trampling on my First Amendment rights, are you, Sergeant Marvia Plum?'

'No, ma'am. Your confidential sources are safe and I'm not planning to subpoena your working notes.'

'That's good. Then we can get along like nice chummy pals. I always got along with the cops in Chicago; why not here?'

'You're from Chicago?'

'A long, long story, darlin'. You want to talk about old Radio Red. Don't blame you. I'd like to know what happened myself.'

'You did a nice piece in the *Mirror*.'

Markham grinned. 'Figured I could grab some extra shekels and spread my byline around your glittering metropolis, Sergeant. Oceana doesn't pay a living wage, but it's better than sitting on my bum waiting for the undertaker.'

Marvia tried hard to keep her professional objectivity. It was hard not to like this woman.

'Well, as we used to say in my days on the saloon beat, your place or mine?' Markham asked.

'How about yours?'

'Fine. My office is around the corner here on Huntington. You know Shaughnessy's Saloon? Sure you do. Come on, let's put something warm under our belts.' She took Marvia by the elbow and steered her toward the parking lot exit. She called back over her shoulder, 'Hey Loman — if Nikki Klein wants me, I'm in my private executive suite with the Sarge here.'

Maude Markham ordered Shaughnessy's specialty, an Irish coffee in a massive mug. Marvia told the bartender to leave the whiskey out of hers. She was on duty and she took the rules seriously. She watched Maude Markham lower the level of her drink with a single swig, then asked if she was a KRED old-timer. From her looks, she could go back to the days of the legendary four founders.

'Not me, darlin'. I just hit this burg a little while ago. Worked all my life for one paper or another in Chicago. I got sick of writing the same stories I'd been writing for forty years, and sick of those icy howlers off the lake. So I packed it in and moved out here.'

The two women found a dark wooden booth. They weren't the only customers in the place, somewhat surprisingly for this hour of the morning. Marvia said, 'Did Bob Bjorner have any enemies around the station? Would anyone there want him dead?'

Markham grinned. 'Anybody there *not* want him dead, is more like it. Bobby was not Mr. Congeniality.'

'Okay, just for the record. Where were you when Bjorner died?'

'He was supposed to go on the air at three p.m. and he died right there in front of his mike, right? I was at city hall interviewing council member Sherry Hanson. If you need verification, I'm sure she'll remember the meeting. She threw me out of her office. When I got back to KRED the yellow tape was up.'

'She threw you out? Why?'

'I wish I could prove it. I think she's mad that I got a job at KRED. She liked the old guard better. Sees me as part of Sun Mbolo's reactionary gang. Hell, sis, I just went over to city hall to ask her about the new Hall of Justice. We started talking about KRED, and the next thing I knew, I was out of there. Bitch!'

'All right, I'll check with her office if necessary. But look — what's this about people disliking Bjorner? I mean, he just came in and did his show every afternoon, isn't that right?'

'Why do people kill each other, sis?'

'Most killings are family killings. Boyfriends and girlfriends and married couples and parents killing children. And acquaintance killings. Friends fall out; business partners.'

'What else?'

'Drugs. Turf wars. And people wanting to get rid of witnesses before they can testify.'

'Good. What else?'

'Wrong-place-wrong-time killings. Muggings that go wrong. Holdups where the victim resists and pulls a weapon out from behind a counter.'

'Then who's your candidate for the

Bjorner killing? You're sure it was a killing, right, not an accident or a do-it-yourself exit job?'

'Coroner hasn't issued his finding yet.'

'Gotcha.'

'What?'

'Where I come from, it means a wink's as good as a nod. Now, you told me, darlin', family first. Who is there?'

'Maude, I'd really like to tell you this, but I can't compromise an ongoing investigation.'

'Okay,' Maude said, 'suppose I tell you. Everybody knows that Red was a widower — well, something like one, anyhow — and he lived with his little brother Herbie.'

Marvia grunted. 'How did they get along?'

'Apparently they liked each other okay. But you never know, do you?'

The bartender signaled. Maude Markham hoisted herself out of the booth and swapped their empties for two fresh mugs.

'Anybody else?' Markham asked. 'You said that drug deals come in second around here. Radio Red wasn't a doper.'

'He wasn't?'

'Not so's I knew.'

Marvia almost told her about the drug cocktail in Bjorner's ashtray, but she restrained herself. Could she give Markham something harmless and get something useful back for it? 'There was an ashtray on the table where he was sitting when he died.'

Markham shook her head. 'KRED is smoke-free.'

'Do you have any reason to believe that Robert Bjorner was involved in drug transactions? Either for his personal use or as a dealer?'

'I didn't even know he was a doper.'

'And I didn't say he was, either, Maude. All right?'

'I always protect my sources.'

'Okay. Me too. But you still haven't told me why Bjorner was disliked at KRED.'

'He was an old-line Stalinist. Last of the breed. Marx was right, Lenin was right, Trotsky was wrong, Bukharin this, Dzerzhinsky that, Stalin, Molotov, Vishinsky, Mao Zedong, Ho Chi Minh. Nobody could disagree; he'd tear into them like a Baptist preacher who caught a kid looking at a skin mag. Hey, even with people who *agreed* with him, he'd always find some fine point to pick, to show how much he knew. The other guy was always wrong.'

Marvia frowned. She'd heard the last-surviving-Stalinist line from Margarita Horowitz; Markham confirmed the story. But was that enough? 'So he was irritating. We're talking about don't invite him to your barbecue. We're not talking about murder.'

'You didn't know Red.'

'Fair enough.' There was the woman who murdered her husband because he squeezed the toothpaste tube at the wrong end. But this killing was too well-planned for that kind of impulsive, irrational violence. There must be something more to it than Bjorner's dogmatic conduct. And his last script opened with a quotation from Khrushchev's secret speech on Stalin's crimes. If Bjorner had been the last of the old-time Stalinists, why was he quoting that speech? Ed Florio said it was all metaphor, a symbolic attack on Sun Mbolo. Crazy as it sounded, Ms. Mbolo kept looking like a prime suspect.

Marvia checked her watch. 'Got to get rolling.' She settled with Markham for her two coffees and left a dollar tip. They walked west on Huntington and turned south on BJB. Maude Markham headed into KRED for the second time that morning, and Marvia Plum stepped into Bix's Wax Cylinder. She identified herself and asked to speak with the owner.

The tall, almost skeletal man behind the counter offered a lugubrious look. 'I guess that's me.'

Marvia had heard that scratchy-whispery voice before. This man was the disc jockey on the late-night music show.

'I'm the owner, the chief buyer, sales consultant, bookkeeper, and floor-sweeper.'

'Nobody else works here?'

A shrug. 'Not much money in this business.'

Marvia nodded. 'I'm investigating the death of Robert Bjorner. I need to talk with you for a while.' She handed him a business card and he studied it, then slipped it into a drawer behind the heavy glass-topped counter.

'Let's begin with your name.' She knew damned well who he was, but she wanted to start the interview with a blank slate.

'Leon Bismarck Beiderbecke, a.k.a. Little Bix.' He was six-four at least.

'Why little?'

'I was named for the famous Bix. We were third cousins; he died years before I was born. When I was a kid I played cornet and piano. Learned all his solos. Everybody called me Little Bix. Unfortunately, I didn't have his talent. I got a few gigs on the strength of my name, decided it was all a shuck, and went in the wax business instead.'

Marvia looked around the store. 'What do you do for KRED?'

'I run *The Wax Mine*.' When Marvia didn't respond to that he said, 'I spin old records. Rarities going back to 1900 or before. But mostly from the 1920s through the '40s. When Elvis swivel-hipped in the front door, I black-bottomed out the back.'

'Got it. What are your hours at KRED?'

'Two to four a.m., five nights a week.'

'That's a ten-hour week. Do they pay you much for that?'

'You don't know much about KRED, do you, lady?'

'You tell me.'

He raised a hand and gestured around his store. 'You see this? People will pay good prices for old recordings, even if they can get the same material on CD. Sometimes, *especially* if they can get it on CD. Reissues spark interest in old material, and people start sniffing around for original pressings.' He came around from behind the counter and stood over a rack of twelve-inch albums, then pulled one from the rack. 'You see this, lady? *The Freewheelin' Bob Dylan*, Columbia, 1963.'

'I know it.'

'Bet you didn't know the first pressing was destroyed. Never circulated. Dylan was lined up to do an Ed Sullivan show and the network boobs wanted to check his material. He was gonna do 'The

Talkin' John Birch Blues.' They wouldn't let him do the song 'cause they didn't want to offend all those right-wing crackers and wackos. He got so mad, he made Columbia pull the LP and change half the tracks. Made 'em melt down the whole first pressing . . . only not quite.' He had a gleam in his eye. 'Couple of copies got out. Lot of ignorant people, even Dylan collectors, think they have the first pressing of *Freewheelin'*, but they don't. Far as anybody knew, even dealers, there were just a handful of copies of the *real* first pressing. All in mono. They're worth a fortune. Ten, twelve grand easy. Then somebody turned up a stereo copy. Not in the best shape. Still, think of it — a unique Dylan. What a piece for a collector! If you can get hold of a *Freewheelin'* with 'Talkin' John Birch Blues,' buy it for any price — you'll make a fortune in a few years.'

'Where were you when Bob Bjorner died?'

He slipped the album back into the rack and put the counter between himself and Marvia once more. She wasn't happy about that; she didn't know what he had back there. Maybe a firearm.

'When was that?' he asked.

'Last Monday. He was just about to go on the air.'

'Oh, I would have been here in the shop, then. Radio Red went on at three o'clock every day, didn't he? Not my cup of tea; I didn't really pay much attention.'

'You were here in your store? You're sure?'

'I got to earn a living, lady. What I started to tell you before, you wouldn't listen. KRED didn't pay me a nickel. Ever. They pay the managers and the technical staff, but most of the talent is volunteers.'

'You mean you drag yourself in there every morning at two o'clock and work for the next two hours, and you don't get paid anything?'

'For the love of my music. And it doesn't hurt my business, either. People come in all the time — 'I heard you on KRED. I heard you playing this fabulous music, something like, kind of jazzy, only it sounded like Jewish wedding music.'

And I tell 'em, sure, that was Klezmer, I've got a whole rack of the stuff, and they get excited and plunk down a few bills for CDs. That's how I make a living. That, plus servicing the serious collectors' market, but that's a whole other thing.'

'And you were in the store at three p.m., Monday last.'

'Yes, that's right. How many times we have to go over it?'

'All right, let's leave that alone. What did you think of Bob Bjorner?'

'I didn't think about him much. His show went on twelve hours out of phase with me; we were never in the studio together. I used to catch little bits of his show once in a while and it bored me.'

'All right. I just had the impression that you didn't like him much. Were you very upset when he died?'

Beiderbecke shrugged his thin, bony shoulders. 'Nope.'

'What did Bjorner think of you?'

'How the heck should I know?'

'You told me he didn't like your show.'

'Look, I'll level with you. Red was a real throwback. He believed in socialist realism. He didn't think that music had any intrinsic value. No art did. Theater, painting, books — everything had to serve the cause of the revolution. You dig? So he really got steamed. Well he used to, years ago. Lately, I just don't think he had the energy. But he used to call up during my show. Sometimes I turn on the request line — not every night, but every now and then — and he'd ream me out for wasting precious air time and deadening the revolutionary conscious-ness of the listening masses. That kind of crap.'

'How did you react to those calls?'

'Depends on how I felt. Sometimes I laughed at him. Sometimes I hung up. Once in a while he'd get to me and I'd give him what-for.'

'Okay, I can see that. You were just trying to play good music — '

'Not just play good music.' He was suddenly red in the face. '*Sharing* great music is as much a sacrament as sex or prayer or peyote. You follow me?'

'But the officers who responded to KRED took the names of everyone in the station at the time of Bob Bjorner's death. Your name was on the list.'

The crane-like figure folded forward across the counter, long arms closing around Marvia Plum like the wings of a great skinny bird.

14

Marvia wished she'd worn her full cop regalia. A quick shot of pepper spray would have done the trick, but she didn't have that with her and she didn't want to escalate all the way to lethal force. She managed to untangle herself from Beiderbecke. Tall as Beiderbecke was, the back edge of the counter caught him at the hip-line and he doubled over the glass. Marvia twisted out of his grasp long enough to get a handhold on him. She walked him around the end of the counter and made him spread his legs until his hands were down to her level. She got him into handcuffs and started him marching toward the front door.

He was complaining and explaining, apologizing for losing his temper and threatening to bring a complaint against her for excessive use of force, all in a jumbled melange. Maybe he was on something. Before they hit the door he dug his heels in and, in that peculiar rasping whisper, asked if he could at least lock up the store. 'They'll steal me blind if I leave it.'

'OK. Where are your keys?'

He dipped his head. 'Right in my pocket.'

Marvia ordered him to stand still while she removed the keys. She drew a sudden breath. 'What the hell is this?' She drew her hand back out of his pocket, holding a small glass pipe. She pushed him ahead of her so she could get a closer look at his hands. She expected to see the telltale darkening of the fingers where a crackhead would clutch his pipe until the flesh was seared. They didn't care, not as long as they were getting their rush. But Bix's delicate bony fingers were as pale as a corpse's.

'That's not my pipe,' he said. 'Look at me, do I look like a crackhead? Come on, you bitch, look me in the face — do I look like a doper? I was just holding it for a friend. Give me a blood test — you'll see, I don't smoke that stuff. You'll see — you put me in jail and wait for me to get the shakes, and I won't!'

'I just want to know, how do you keep functioning? How do you keep your store going, and do a radio show?'

'It's just like I told you, you bitch. I don't use that stuff.'

'I'll bet you don't.' Was he telling the truth? 'You still want me to lock up your store?' He nodded. She extracted the keys from his pocket and locked the front door. Then she led him around the corner and put him into the back of her black-and-white.

She climbed into the front and called in to Dispatch. Then she heard a sound from behind her and turned around. Beiderbecke was leaning against the grille. There were tears running down his cheeks.

'I swear I didn't have anything to do with it. I didn't kill Red. If you'll let me go, I'll — '

Marvia turned to face him through the grille. She pulled the Miranda card from her pocket and performed the ceremony.

He said, 'Never mind, I know you won't let me go.'

'Do you understand your rights?' she persisted.

After a pause, he grated: 'Sure.'

Marvia drove back to the Hall of Justice on McKinley. It took three wearying hours to get Beiderbecke booked into the city jail and the crack pipe booked into evidence, weigh the rocks that turned up in another pocket, run a quick chemical test on them, write up the case, and fill out an application for a search warrant for Bix's Wax Cylinder and for Beiderbecke's home, wherever that was. Beiderbecke insisted that he lived in the back of the store; he had a cot and a propane stove there and he saved money that way.

She ran a warrant check and discovered a couple of minor out-of-state holds, an old Texas conviction for simple possession, paroled after serving one year and wanted for flight, plus a suspended sentence from Riverside County for possession with intent. That was interesting.

Marvia left a voice-mail for Mack Stillman in which she gave him the bare bones of the Beiderbecke bust and suggested that they chat. She wanted to talk with him about Blue Beetle and Acid Alice, really, and about a possible San Remo connection. And about Jamie. She knew that Stillman used snitches all the time. But she also knew that SIB didn't like using juveniles. Youth Services didn't like it either.

Maybe Dorothy Yamura could provide some guidance. Marvia had talked with her about the brainstorming session on the Bjorner case, but Marvia had been so busy she hadn't had time even to set one up, let alone conduct it.

She spent the afternoon studying canvass reports and catching up on paperwork. At dinnertime she downed a sandwich at her desk, washed it down with coffee and kept working. By the time she got out of the Hall of Justice it was pushing eight thirty, and she felt as if she'd been beaten with a baton.

The short drive home along familiar streets became an exhausting journey through alien surroundings. At last she pulled the Mustang into the driveway on

Bonita Street and dragged herself into the house. Jamie was sitting in the kitchen with his headphones on and his Discman on the table, spooning cornflakes into his mouth. He looked up at Marvia, nodded, and kept spooning cornflakes. She signaled him to pull the phones and he complied.

'Didn't Gloria give you dinner?'

He grunted and nodded an affirmative.

'Then what's with the cereal?'

'Bedtime snack.'

Something clicked in Marvia's brain and she made a mental note to revisit the conversation. 'How was school today?' she asked. She was trying desperately to be Mom Marvia, to leave Cop Marvia back at McKinley Avenue, but she wasn't doing very well.

And Jamie wasn't helping. 'Okay.'

'Did you come straight home?'

'Sure.'

'Did you see Hakeem today?'

'Yes.'

Marvia pressed her forehead against the cool enamel side of the refrigerator. She wondered if she felt the same way

218

Leon Beiderbecke had when he had leaned his head against the grille in the black-and-white. She really didn't like him for the Bjorner killing. Bjorner didn't like Beiderbecke's ideas about music, and Beiderbecke didn't like Bjorner's. But Beiderbecke was winning. He was in what Bjorner would have called the capitalist sellout camp. Bjorner had been in line to lose his show, and Beiderbecke was going to keep his. If anyone had reason to become enraged enough to kill, it would have been Bjorner, not Beiderbecke. So why had Bix lied about being at KRED when Radio Red died?

Abruptly Jamie got to his feet. 'I haven't done my homework yet. I better finish up.' He disappeared.

Marvia walked into the living room. Gloria looked up from the television long enough to nod once. What was it about Jamie eating cereal that she wanted to think about? It had something to do with KRED. There were bizarre images in her head — a detective named Nick Train and some kind of Aztec princess, and they were part of a serial.

She clapped her hands so loudly that Gloria flinched, then glared angrily.

Marvia patted her on the shoulder and walked stiff-legged to the front hallway. Something about cereal and a serial and the Radio Red killing. The old adventure serials used to run fifteen-minute episodes, and Robert Bjorner was on a fifteen-minute daily schedule. Just like the old serials. Bjorner worked from a script, and Wilma Ransome had translated Bjorner's final script for her. But you'd think that a man like Radio Red Bob Bjorner would prepare his scripts well ahead of each day's broadcast. Maybe a week at a time, since his show ran as a daily segment of week-long strips. If Bjorner's script for the day he died was the Khrushchev-Stalin speech — or part of it — what was Red planning to talk about for the *rest* of the week?

Herbert Bjorner would know. And even if he didn't, Robert would still have worked ahead, painstakingly punching out his scripts on his Braille typewriter. And where was that? Odds-on, it was in

220

the Bjorner house on Vine Street in north Berkeley.

The TV clicked off in the living room and Gloria Plum emerged. When she saw Marvia she said, 'You just standing there? You coming or going?'

Marvia said, 'Hello, Mom, nice to see you. How was your day?'

'I have things to do.' She disappeared into the bathroom.

Things to do. Marvia looked at her watch. Damn that fool Beiderbecke, and damn her for letting him get into her head. Would Mbolo be home at this time in the evening? She decided to phone. If she got Mbolo's machine, she'd apologize and ask Mbolo to call back in the morning.

But instead of either Mbolo answering the phone or her machine clicking on, Marvia heard the phone simply ring and ring and ring. There was something wrong with that. The hairs on the back of her neck stood up. She wanted to drive straight to Mbolo's house, but she had to live by the same rules as any other cop. She left her car at the Hall of Justice and checked out a black-and-white.

Mbolo lived on Tamalpais Road in the hills above north Berkeley. Marvia found Mbolo's number and pulled to the curb. The house was a Craftsman bungalow, a style popular in Berkeley in the 1920s. Lights glowed behind the large rectangular front window. A small wisp of smoke curled upward from the chimney.

Marvia looked for a doorbell. She couldn't find one, but there was a brass knocker shaped like a bear's head. She raised it and hit the strike-plate. While she waited for Mbolo to respond she turned and surveyed Codornices Park and the Berkeley Rose Garden. Beyond these, the city fell away dramatically to the black face of San Francisco Bay and the glittering lights of the city itself.

She turned back and used the knocker again. There was still no answer. Next she tried the front door, but it was locked. She walked around the house, hoping to find some clue to earlier events, but saw nothing until she reached the rear of the house and found a small concrete stoop two steps above ground level. She climbed to the stoop and saw classic pry-marks on the back door frame. She tried the door and it swung open.

There was little doubt that this was a crime scene. The perp might still be inside Mbolo's house. If Marvia acted fast — and made the right decision — she might prevent a serious crime. If she made the wrong decision, she might compound a tragedy.

She should stay out of the house and call for backup. But something might be happening inside the house right now. The place seemed absolutely quiet. She sprinted back to the cruiser, called in to Dispatch, grabbed a pair of gloves, and yanked them over her hands as she raced back to the house.

She stepped inside and found herself in the kitchen. There were cooking odors in the air. The lids on a couple of pots on the stove were clattering as their contents bubbled. Marvia turned off the gas and the bouncing subsided. She heard music. She drew her Airweight and held it close to her body.

Now there was movement inside the

house. She closed the back door behind her and moved forward. A swinging door separated the kitchen from a small dining room; a wedge of rubber held the door halfway open. Something rustled. She found a wall switch and illuminated the room.

A huge orange cat sat in the middle of a table, washing its paws with an astonishing pink tongue. It looked at Marvia, decided that she was of little interest, and went back to washing.

The dining room opened onto a small foyer. 'Ms. Mbolo?'

No one answered Marvia's call.

The dining room was on her left and a living room on her right. She advanced into the latter. Inexpensive gray shag rug, Mission-style furniture, a couple of paintings on the walls. In one corner an old-fashioned cathedral-top radio played; its dial glowed like gold. The musical selection ended and an announcer identified the station as KRED and gave the time as 9:28 p.m.

A small fire was burning behind the stone-faced hearth. And Sun Mbolo was lying on her back, her eyes open, her African dress torn from her shoulders and hoisted around her waist. The straps of a plain tan brassiere were pulled loose and wrapped around her neck. The shag rug around her was a dreadful reddish-black swamp.

Marvia flinched and gagged, then forced herself to take in the situation. One more look at Mbolo before she acted. The room was lit only by the fire, and Mbolo's skin was even darker than Marvia's; it was hard to distinguish colors. Marvia found a wall switch and moved it with one latex-covered fingertip. Amber lights on a black cast-iron chandelier glowed softly.

Like a crazed ferret, Marvia raced from room to room. No one. No one in Mbolo's walk-in closet. No one waiting behind the shower door. She found Mbolo's answering machine, the plug simply removed from the wall unit. Whoever had done the dreadful things to Mbolo had disconnected the unit.

She returned to the living room and knelt beside Mbolo. Even though she was fairly certain the killer had left the scene, she kept her S&W in her hand. Now she could make out multiple chest wounds, each smaller around than the shaft of a common pencil. She'd seen this kind of wound before, in photographs, but never in the flesh. They were ice-pick punctures. She counted almost twenty of them. She couldn't tell how deep they were, but they looked severe. Why had they caused so little bleeding? There were puzzles here that the coroner would have to solve, but Marvia was able to make some educated guesses.

She looked at Mbolo's legs. A probable rape, attempted or completed. She wondered again why there was so little blood on the body when there was so much on the carpet. The greatest amount of spilled blood had spattered and pooled near Mbolo's waist. Marvia knelt just beyond the red-black swamp and studied the body. She was tempted to raise the torso and find out what lay beneath. She had an idea what she would find if she did that, but she resisted the temptation. That was the coroner's business, and if she moved the body she could disturb evidence.

She returned to the cruiser again and called the watch commander. The watch commander was Abe Craigie, the department's chief cynic. But he was a solid old-timer, a first-rate cop. He was aware of her earlier call and told her that a patrol car was en route. She told him that he'd better send an evidence van and the coroner's wagon, as there was a body in the house, an apparent murder and possible rape. And no indication that the perpetrator was still nearby.

Craigie said, 'Okay, Plum, you know the drill. Secure the scene.'

Marvia scouted out the house. Five rooms; she'd already been through the kitchen, dining room, and the living room where Sun Mbolo lay. The other rooms were bedrooms; one furnished as such, the other converted to a home-office. Those rooms plus the bathroom, the foyer, half a dozen closets. No sign of any living thing save herself and the orange cat.

She heard a thump and whirled. She

drew her S&W Airweight and followed the sound.

The orange cat had jumped off the dining room table and was sniffing at Sun Mbolo. It stepped in the bloody swamp around her and drew back, looking at its paw in alarm. It sat on its haunches and proceeded to wash off the offending blood.

Marvia touched her fingertips to Sun Mbolo's carotid. She couldn't feel any pulse. She knelt beside Mbolo's head and bent to hold her cheek and ear close to her face. No sound of breath, no feeling of exhaled air. She laid her hand on Mbolo's forehead. It felt warm, almost as warm as life. But was that because she was only recently dead, or because she lay near an open hearth? Marvia felt the victim's cheek further from the fire. It was noticeably cooler than the side she had previously touched.

She heard sirens approaching and turned to see roof lights flashing red and blue. When she opened the front door she faced Zack Rider, a longtime sergeant she knew well. He said, 'What have you got?'

'Homicide, one cadaver in the living room.' She indicated the direction. 'Perp or perps have probably fled — I checked the house and couldn't find anyone. Good idea to have a couple of your people recheck. And get people into the neighborhood in case they're still nearby.'

Rider's radio was crackling and he was talking into it. He turned around and gave instructions to his people, then asked Marvia if she was certain the victim was dead. She nodded and led Rider into the living room. 'Victim is Sun Mbolo, general manager at KRED.'

Rider turned in a circle, surveying the room, before he knelt beside the remains of Sun Mbolo. He was broad-shouldered with skin almost as dark as Marvia's, and wavy steel-gray hair. He'd field-trained Marvia when she joined the force.

Without touching the body, he peered at Mbolo's thighs, moved his hand as if to pull her dress down and give her some degree of privacy and dignity, then held himself back. He said, 'Where are her panties?' He pointed at Mbolo's neck. 'She was wearing a bra. She'd be wearing

229

panties too, wouldn't she?'

'Right. Maybe the perp is a souvenir-hunter.'

'That's all we need.' He heaved himself back to his feet. 'How well do you know this neighborhood?'

'You thinking about flight? No bus lines near here, but they could have parked and driven away afterwards.'

'Let's see what the canvass turns up. And where are the weapons?'

'What weapons?'

Marvia pointed to the almost bloodless chest wounds. 'Classic ice-pick job, almost certainly postmortem. I don't understand the brassiere around her throat. Just craziness. Looks like the work of a woman-hater.'

Rider frowned. 'He strangled her, raped her, then stabbed her? The son of a bitch.'

They were interrupted by the arrival of the evidence crew. Marvia was in charge of the site and pointed them at the cadaver. One of the technicians asked, 'Anybody touch anything?' Marvia said she'd touched the body just enough to make certain that Mbolo was dead.

Soon the techs were sketching, shooting photos and hunting for scraps. When the coroner's squad arrived, they finally lifted Sun Mbolo and revealed the source of the bloody swamp. By a combination of flickering firelight and amber glow from the chandelier, Marvia could make out a two- to three-inch slice in the fabric of Mbolo's dress. That must have been the first wound, inflicted from the rear. From its location, it had probably severed the victim's spine and rendered her immobile from the hips downward. If the attacker then extracted the knife and Mbolo had fallen supine on the rug, she would have bled to death from the back wound. The rape had been committed on the dead or dying victim. The chest wounds, then, would have been delivered postmortem, and consequently caused very little bleeding.

To Rider she said, 'That's why I think the strangulation is gratuitous. He used that big knife. He could have ditched the weapons somewhere in the house, maybe outside in the bushes. Maybe he still has them.' She inhaled deeply, suddenly short of breath. 'Wait a minute.' She jerked a thumb toward the fireplace.

Rider joined her. The broad-bladed kitchen knife and the slim ice-pick were visible in the middle of the fire. 'Quick!' Marvia exclaimed. 'Let's fish those things out of there and see if we can get anything off 'em. I doubt it, but let's try. Zack, get one of those evidence techs to pull the knife and pick out of there.' She was the first officer on the scene, and even though Rider was senior to her, this was going to be her case. But that didn't stop Rider from asking how she had discovered the crime.

'Mbolo called me at home last night. She wanted to talk to me about the Bjorner killing. You up to speed on that one?'

'I've heard about it, sure. Who hasn't?'

'Said she wanted to talk to me about Bjorner. She wanted me to come up here, but I put her off — and now, goddamn it, somebody did this to her.'

Rider raised his eyebrows. 'You think it was your fault? If you'd come last night she'd be alive now?'

Marvia didn't answer.

'Can't think that way, Sarge. You can't change it, you can't fix it, and you can't run the world.'

'And this is just a job, right?'

She remembered what he'd told her when they discussed the question years ago, riding in a black-and-white after she'd graduated from the academy. She'd felt wobbly inside, and had asked Rider, and he'd turned philosopher. 'It's a responsibility,' he'd said. 'I don't go along with officers who say it's just a job. It means a hell of a lot more than driving a cab or selling popcorn at the movies. But don't try and carry the world on your shoulders, Marvia. You can't do it. Nobody can do it. You'll crack up if you try.'

A patrol officer entered the house and approached Marvia and Rider. Marvia halted him with a gesture. 'What do you have for me?'

'First neighbor is an old lady who's kinda deaf. She didn't seem to understand there'd been a crime here. I got out of there.'

'Okay, then what?'

'Next house was occupied by two males, one white, one Asian. I think I detected a cannabis odor but I didn't pursue that.'

'Good, right, what then?'

'They said a VW van went past a couple of times last night and they saw it again tonight. Real old, from the '70s, you know? With flowers and stuff.'

'And?'

'And one of them said some guy was just cruising up and down Tamalpais.'

'Okay.' Marvia shot a glance at Zack Rider. He was listening intently to the officer. 'These citizens have nothing better to do than watch the traffic cruise by their house?'

'I wouldn't know, Sergeant. I guess maybe they were smoking pot and they got stoned and came outside to look at the view from here.'

'Okay, fine. Did they notice anything else about this van, except that it was old and that it went past several times?'

'Well, the Asian guy, he was the one who saw it mainly. And his friend thought maybe he was tripping or something because he got upset, and he said he asked him what he was upset about, and he thought there was something wrong with the guy driving the van.' He stopped and took a deep breath and then he resumed. 'So he stayed there, and when the guy went by again, he was headed south on Tamalpais, so the driver's side was on the east side of the vehicle, toward the house. And the Asian guy thought the driver had bugs crawling on him, big blue cockroaches or something. His friend took him back in the house, and he said he thought maybe he needed some of that tranquilizer stuff they use for acid-heads or something. I mean, big blue cockroaches on your face — man, talk about a bum trip!'

15

Marvia struggled to finish her paperwork at McKinley Avenue. She'd slugged down coffee to keep going. This was going to mean another autopsy to attend. She had learned to deal with that experience, but she still hated watching the procedure and hearing the sounds of the autopsy room.

Even though the description of the VW van was minimal — if only the two men had got a license plate number! — she put out a teletype on it. She thought of sending one out on Blue Beetle, but decided that the word of a hallucinating drug-user wouldn't get her anywhere.

One thought crept up and screamed into her face: *If you'd gone to Tamalpais Road twenty-four hours sooner, Sun Mbolo might be alive tonight.* And whatever it was that Mbolo wanted to tell her might have untied the Gordian knot that had formed around the Bjorner killing.

At length she took the hottest shower she could stand and dressed and drove to Bonita Street. She stood outside the house, praying that Gloria and Jamie were both still asleep. She was afraid that if she had to say as much as 'hello, good night,' she would start to scream.

The house was silent, and she breathed a sigh of relief. The staircase was as steep as a mountain. She climbed it and crawled into bed, but stared at the ceiling, unable to sleep yet too weary to move. Sun Mbolo's bloody cadaver lay on the gray shag rug. The image of her pulled-up dress and her spread thighs was more disturbing than the wounds in her chest and back or even her dead, staring eyes.

Marvia tried to think of Leon Beiderbecke as the perpetrator, but it didn't hang together. How could an addict keep his life together as Beiderbecke apparently did, running a business and maintaining a two-hour radio show five nights a week? Maybe he was telling the truth. She hadn't even bothered to ask

Bix whose pipe and rocks they were. She should have done that. Bad cop work.

She struggled out of bed and called the city jail. Sure, Beiderbecke was in a holding cell, sleeping like an innocent babe. Marvia told the jailer to hold him in the morning, not ship him over to court. Maybe they could work something out.

All right, and what about the driver of the van on Tamalpais? The canvass had turned up the Asian acid-head, if that was what he was, who had seen the driver with blue cockroaches on his face. That had to be Solomon San Remo's one-time acquaintance Steve Insetta, aka Blue Beetle. Blue Beetle and Acid Alice connected to Solomon San Remo connected to KRED connected to both Robert Bjorner and Sun Mbolo.

Marvia sat down on the edge of her bed. She rolled onto her side, hit the 'sleep' button on the radio, and found herself back in the jungle of Oaxaca with Nick Train and Tina Carter.

She was surprised, when she woke a couple of hours later, at how well she had slept. She phoned Mack Stillman at the office and set up a meeting. When she got to McKinley she headed straight to Narcotics and found him in SIB.

He looked up and winked. 'What can old Uncle Stillman do for you this morning?'

'I have a feeling your pal Blue Beetle is involved in more than dope, Inspector.' She told him about the Mbolo murder, and the witness who had seen the van and the driver with the cockroaches on his face.

Stillman nodded in agreement. 'Sounds like a tripper's version of Blue Beetle. You get any response on the van?'

'Not yet.'

'Well — ' Stillman spread his hands. ' — what can I do for you, anyhow?'

'First, some more info on Beetle and Alice. I already talked to Solomon San Remo up at Q. He told me a little about them.'

'He have their full names?'

'Solly told me that Blue Beetle was Steve Insetta. He didn't say anything about Alice.'

'Yeah, Alice Gonser. Interesting pair.

College sweethearts, of a sort. He was an ethnobotanist working out of U of Oregon. Just loved unusual plant life. She was a marine biologist out of UC San Diego. They met in a village on the Amazon River, isn't that romantic? He was studying the plants, she was studying the fish. Next thing you know, they're sharing a sleeping bag or whatever the hell they use there in the jungle.'

Marvia waved her hand. 'I don't see how that gets them to Ho Chi Minh Park selling dope to school kids.'

'They sampled the wonders of coca and a basketful of other goodies there in South America, and they came back here to spread the gospel of psychedelic salvation. One thing leads to another and next thing you know, Mr. Insetta and Ms. Gonser are transformed into Blue Beetle and Acid Alice.'

'But they sell *guns* to kids!'

'You want to challenge their dealers' license, Marvia? What the heck do you want me to do? Intelligence says that they got into gun-running in South America, too. The cold war was still going on, and

Castro was sending in Kalishnikovs, the CIA was sending in M-16s, and if you were willing to take some risks and grease a few palms you could bring in anything you wanted and take out anything you wanted. Guns in, cocaine out. With a nice profit margin at both ends of the transaction.'

'What the hell are these guys doing in the playground?' Marvia demanded. 'If the Brazilians didn't put 'em away, why didn't Uncle Sam nab them when they got back, the minute they stepped off the airplane? Why don't the Feds grab 'em now, for that matter?'

'Insetta and Gonser have good timing. They flew into Miami the same week that Gorbachev got kidnapped. You remember that? State Department went nuts, and all the airports went into sniffer mode for any damn thing that might happen. And by that time, who cares about a couple of ex-hippie drug dealers coming home after their cruise up the Amazon?'

'But it's not like they're in hiding.'

'Of course not. But the Feds don't give a damn. Insetta and Gonser are nothing but a footnote to an old story. *I* care about them because they're dirtying up my town, but they know how to use cut-outs, they play a cautious game, and I haven't been able to take 'em yet. But before I retire from this job, I'm going to retire them from theirs.' There was a silence. Then Stillman said, 'You still have that confidential source?'

Marvia hesitated. 'Maybe. But I think there might be a better way.' She proceeded to tell him about Leon Bismarck 'Little Bix' Beiderbecke.

Stillman stood up. 'You say this guy is still upstairs? Let's go see your special amigo.'

They wound up in an interview room, Beiderbecke in his jail coveralls and handcuffs, Marvia Plum and Mack Stillman wearing civvies. Stillman had set up a tape recorder. He said, 'Mr. Beiderbecke, I'll remove your handcuffs if you'll behave yourself.'

Beiderbecke held up his hands and Stillman removed the cuffs and clipped them to a belt loop on his pants. Beiderbecke sat back down and glared at

Marvia. His pale hands were steady. He rasped, 'See, bitch, I told you.'

Stillman pulled out a Miranda card and went through the ritual for Beiderbecke's sake. Beiderbecke acknowledged that he understood his rights. Stillman asked if Beiderbecke minded him recording the conversation. Beiderbecke grumbled but eventually agreed.

'Good. Now, let's examine this situation. Assaulting an officer — '

'I'm sorry. She jerked my chain, I was nervous and tired, and I flipped out. I didn't hurt anybody, and I'm sorry for what I did. Can we just leave it at that?'

Stillman looked at Marvia. She took the cue. 'That's very nice, Mr. Beiderbecke, that you apologized to me. But suppose I accept your apology and don't press that charge. Even if I overlook the assault on an officer, you were in possession of illegal drug paraphernalia and a sizable Baggie full of rocks.'

'I told you yesterday, Sergeant, it wasn't my stuff. Look, you guys took a urine sample from me; you must have got the report by now. And I don't have any withdrawal jitters, nothing. So you know I'm not a user.'

'Whose material was it?' Marvia asked him.

'It was some guy came in the store. I didn't know him. He said the cops were after him and he was scared of getting busted. He was already out on parole, and if he got popped for possession he was in deep trouble.'

Stillman ran his hand through his gray hair. 'This isn't worth anything, Mr. Beiderbecke. I don't see anything here, do you, Sergeant?'

'No, Inspector.'

'This looks like a good bust to me. I think Mr. Beiderbecke will get an escort over to the court, then he'll either make bail or take a bus ride out to Santa Rita.'

Beiderbecke stood up. 'Okay. Simple possession. You guys can't scare me. I'll walk. Why are you wasting your time?'

Marvia leaned forward. 'You didn't tell me anything about Riverside County, Bix.'

'That was a bum rap. That was planted evidence. You know how those southern

California cops are.'

'And Texas?'

'Simple grass possession. They wouldn't even waste the air fare on that.'

'Isn't that funny, Inspector Stillman? We'd better get the computer wizards to check our system. I put in the inquiry and I got back possession with intent to sell, cocaine, heroin and meth.'

She looked up into Beiderbecke's gaunt face. He was sweating heavily and there was a tremor in his hands. 'What is this, withdrawal after all?'

'No way. I told you, check the urine. I'm clean. I don't use illegal substances.'

Another quick exercise in cop-telepathy between Marvia and Stillman. Then Stillman said, 'You'd better tell me who gave you the pipe and rocks, then.'

'It was somebody I knew in southern California. I was running a record store and I did a DJ show on the Oceana station in San Diego, KOCN. She used to hang out with musicians and some dopers, and she volunteered at KOCN. We got high a few times together. I didn't see her for years, you know, and then she walks into the Wax Cylinder and asks if I'll hold a couple things for her.'

'Why?' Marvia asked him.

'She had an appointment, she said. She was going to talk to Sun Mbolo at KRED. I didn't know she even knew her, but she said she wanted to get a show on KRED. Fat chance — Mbolo would have kicked her out on her butt. Mbolo's this puritan Ethiopian broad, very uptight.'

He doesn't know that Mbolo is dead, Marvia thought. *Or he wants us to think he doesn't know.* She didn't react.

Stillman laid his hands flat on the table. 'Who was it, Mr. Beiderbecke? Do you want to go back to Texas, or do you want to help me out?'

'What's in it for me if I tell you?'

'You'll walk out of here, but we'll still have a string on you. That's what it will mean.'

Beiderbecke said, 'Alice Gonser.'

16

Herbert Bjorner's phone rang for a long time. At last Marvia heard the receiver lifted and heard his voice. 'Yeah.'

'Mr. Bjorner, this is Sergeant Plum. You remember, I'm investigating your brother's death?'

'Right, Sergeant.' She listened to him wheezing for a while, then he asked, 'What's new, Sergeant? What have you learned?'

'I was wondering, Mr. Bjorner, how far ahead Robert worked. His show was on KRED daily, is that correct?'

'Lately. They kept changing it.'

'Yes. But do you know his work methods? Did he do each day's script, say, the night before? Or the morning of the broadcast?'

'He used to work over weekends. He had a five-day strip, Monday through Friday. He worked weekends and had his scripts for the week ready by Monday.'

'Mr. Bjorner, are you going to be home for a while? Could I come by and see you again?'

'Sure, why not. I ain't going nowhere.'

Marvia checked her messages and teletype traffic before heading to Bjorner's house in north Berkeley. A gem of a multiple hit on the van that had been spotted near Sun Mbolo's house. Bay Area Rapid Transit police had found a vehicle matching the description from Mbolo's tripping neighbor. It was abandoned in the parking lot at the Richmond station and it stuck out like a sore thumb. When they ran a check on the tag, it came up registered in Riverside County. The BART police managed to contact the registered owner and they learned that he had abandoned the van a long time ago, and didn't want it back.

Marvia was assembling pieces. Here was another. And it got better. The BART cops towed the van and checked its contents. And they found bloodstains in the van. Bloodstains, a couple of empty liquor bottles, half a dozen marijuana roaches . . . and a pair of bloody latex gloves. They were holding the van and the items found in it, including the blood. What did BPD want them to do with it?

Marvia checked the name of the contact officer on the teletype. She phoned over to BART and talked to the officer. Sure, BART PD would keep the van impounded, and sure, they'd send the items out to San Leandro to be analyzed, and they'd have the lab send copies of all the reports to Sergeant M. Plum at BPD.

Marvia pulled the cruiser to the curb at the Bjorner house on Vine Street. She climbed the steps to the front door. Herb Bjorner answered, clad in a huge shirt that hung past his knees and khaki shorts. He wore sandals, and he hadn't shaved since Marvia first met him outside the KRED building just hours after his brother's death. He didn't smell too great, either. Maybe Robert's death had hit Herbert hard and he just didn't have enough interest in life to take care of himself.

He waved her in, and led the way to the same sitting room they'd used on her previous visit. He walked slowly, his ponderous weight precariously balanced. Then he lowered himself carefully onto the couch.

'Could you show me your brother's workroom?' Marvia said.

Bjorner closed his eyes. 'I wish you'd asked me that before I sat down here.' He struggled to his feet, then launched himself on another walking tour, signaling Marvia to follow.

They proceeded through an arched doorway and a heavy wooden door fitted with antique-style iron hinges and horizontal flanges. It creaked when Bjorner swung it open. He reached aside and flicked a light switch. The bulbs that illuminated the room were feeble, and there were no windows. The air smelled stale.

'How did he get anything done in here?' asked Marvia as she looked around.

'He was nearly blind, you know. At first, after the war, he could see pretty well. But the older he got, his sight got worse and worse. Lately, he just knew his way around. He could find anything, even in pitch darkness.' When Herbert spoke of his brother, animation returned to his manner. 'He liked dim light better than bright light. He said bright light hurt his eyes. He used to wear dark glasses whenever he went out in the daytime, even on a dim day. He said he could see better in a very dim light than a bright one.'

'That's his typewriter?'

Bjorner followed Marvia's indication. 'That's it.'

'A Braille typewriter? I've never seen one before. Did it print out in regular type, as well?'

'No. Just Braille.'

Marvia turned. 'Where are the rest of his scripts — the other four for the week? You told me he prepared a week's scripts in advance.'

'I don't know. Maybe they're at KRED.' He wasn't focusing very well.

'He only had the one in with him in Studio B. Did he have a producer who might hold his scripts for the week?'

'No producer. Not since Anitra died.'

'Anitra Colón?'

Herbert smiled, a peculiar exaggerated smile.

'Someone else mentioned her to me, Mr. Bjorner. She was his common-law wife, wasn't she?'

'Life partner, they called it. Didn't believe in marriage.' He giggled, wobbled, and steadied himself with one hand against the wall.

'She was his producer, then, until her death?'

'Yeah. Three, no, four years ago. Hit by a truck. You know Huntington Way? You know a place there called Shaughnessy's? Three of us went in there for a drink after the Radio Red show one time. Bob had an hour show then. 'Nitra went outside to put a coin in the parking meter and some scab truck driver going past lost control of his truck and ran up on the curb and killed her. *Wham!* Didn't think Bob was going to make it after that, but he put everything he had into KRED.'

'Could he see, then?'

'Less than he could before, more than he could later on. He never went blind, see, that's the point. His vision just faded and faded.'

'The scripts,' Marvia reminded him.

He ignored the prompt. 'See, you have to understand that about KRED. Few people there are professionals, you know? Or it's their hobby, a few of 'em. But most of 'em — they don't have no other life. Bob had a cause. Beiderbecke — now there's a character. He promotes his store on KRED. No commercials, see, but he gets his message across. But most of 'em — you know Dayton?'

Marvia waited.

'Lon Dayton, the OTR guy — you know, old-time radio. I know that guy. He's on some kind of, he told me, a stipend. Aid to the hopelessly bewildered. He rents a crummy little room off of University; hangs out in the library, cadges movie passes from KRED, eats canned beans, goes to free meals in church basements, gets his clothes out of free boxes. It's a big day for him when he can afford a new thrift-shop outfit.' He paused and caught his breath, as much as he could ever catch his breath. 'See, the poor guy is a nobody. You never met him, did you? No. You wouldn't give him the time of day out on the street. But every night for thirty minutes or an hour he's a big man. He's Lon Dayton, the King of OTR. His room is — '

'Have you seen his room?'

'He invited me up a couple of times. Full of thousands of tapes — old adventure shows, comedies, soap operas, even old news broadcasts. He's got *Superman, Jack Benny, Myrt 'n' Marge*. He can put on the news for Pearl Harbor, Roosevelt's death, Kennedy's assassination, the first moon landing, the fall of the Berlin Wall. He's the King of OTR, the Master of Time and Space, the Lord of Laughter and Tears. You ought to hear the things he calls himself.' He paused, panting. Then he shrugged. 'Then he checks out of KRED and goes home to his crummy room and eats beans for dinner and listens to his tapes all night. Sometimes he fills in, gets a special block of time, does an OTR marathon. Twenty-four hours solid, *I Love a Mystery*. Whenever KRED gets a hole in their schedule, Lon jumps in with a tape. See, that's his life. KRED.'

That answered one question that had been bothering Marvia: Why had she heard one of Dayton's adventure tapes early in the morning instead of late at night? But that was another matter. She made one more try. 'The scripts — may I look for them here, Mr. Bjorner?'

'I'll just sit down if you don't mind.'

'What happened after Anitra died?'

'Bobby never had no other producer. Said he didn't need none. He just walked into the studio with his script and went on the air. They gave him a board op and that was the only producer he ever needed.'

'Where did he get the food he was eating when he died?'

'I dropped him off. I wouldn't know.'

Marvia knew that the food had been in Bara Miyako containers, but that didn't prove it had come from Bara Miyako. 'Where did he get his drugs? He was using drugs when he died.'

'Drugs? He never did at home. I wouldn't know. Somebody at KRED?'

'Did your brother know Solomon San Remo? Do you know him?'

'Ran a nightclub on University. Not my crowd.'

'How about Stephen Insetta?'

'No.'

'Alice Gonser?'

'Never heard of her.'

Marvia turned her full attention to sifting through the papers on Robert Bjorner's desk and in the drawers beneath the Braille typewriter. *This must be what a writer's desk is like — complete chaos*, she thought. Crumpled and discarded sheets of paper. Pieces of paper with huge, crayon-like scrawls on them. Of course, with his very poor vision, Radio Red would use such markings. *TUE 1, TUE 2, TUE 3*, And *WED 1, WED 2, WED 3*. Each series of pages marked with a day and a page number.

Marvia riffled through the papers, assembling her bundle. She had found Radio Red's scripts for the rest of the week. Monday was nothing but an excerpt from Khrushchev's anti-Stalin speech. Radio Red had never delivered that script, but it didn't seem especially important. Hardly reason to kill. But what was in the pages he had planned to use the rest of the fatal week?

'Mr. Bjorner, may I take these papers with me? They're in Braille, and I can have them converted into readable type.'

'You take 'em. I can't read that stuff. Maybe there's something good in there, hey?' He giggled.

She thanked him and wrote out a receipt for the pages, then asked if she might use his telephone and called Wilma Ransome, who agreed to work on the scripts right away. Afterward, she walked back down the steps to her black-and-white. Before she started the engine, she sealed the scripts in an evidence bag and carefully marked it. Then she headed for the computer science building.

Wilma Ransome accepted the Braille scripts. She turned her sightless eyes toward Marvia and grinned. 'More fancy evidence stuff? I suppose you'll want me to lock these things up again.'

'Yes. These might be evidence, or they might just be interesting background material, I don't know. If in doubt, take precautions.'

'Fair enough.' She felt the envelope, measuring its thickness and weight with her hands. 'Four times as much material as the first batch.'

'Right.'

'Not to worry. Once the old cruncher revs up, you can still get your output first thing in the a.m.'

'Thanks. And please — be careful with these documents.'

Marvia phoned police headquarters and asked for Lieutenant Yamura. She gave her a capsule version of the case and made her move, setting up her brain-storming session. Yamura gave her a time the following day and Marvia took it. Then she called the desk and asked a civilian admin tech to reserve a briefing room and to invite the people on a list that Marvia read to her.

Finally she checked the directory of KRED personnel she'd got from the station and found Lon Dayton. The directory gave an address on McGee Avenue and a phone number, which she dialed. She got an answering machine that treated her to a minute-long recording of radio sound effects and told her to scream for help and the King of OTR would fly to her rescue. She left her number at police headquarters. Then she drove back to Barbara Jordan Boulevard and parked in front of KRED.

Jessie Loman waved hello when she entered the station. Marvia said, 'Just the woman I want to see. I need to get in touch with Lon Dayton. He doesn't answer his phone.' Even as she spoke, she felt a cold tingle.

Jessie Loman tilted her yellow beret. 'You're in luck — he's in editing room three. That's right upstairs.' She gave Marvia directions.

Editing room three looked a lot like an old-style phone booth with a rubber gasket around the door as a sound-seal. Lon Dayton had the look of an overaged adolescent. He crouched over a tape deck, hitting buttons and spinning reels backward and forward. Every now and then he would stop the tape, pull the ribbon out from among the capstans, slide it into an editing bar, and perform an arcane act with razor blade and adhesive tape.

Marvia rapped on the glass with a coin and Dayton looked up. He wore glasses with thick lenses and black plastic frames. Marvia showed her badge and he looked first astonished, then frightened, then delighted. He signaled her without moving from his seat. There was barely room for Marvia to stand beside Dayton's swivel chair.

'Listen to this,' he said. He hit a button on the editing deck and sound poured from concealed speakers.

The makers of delicious Ohio Bars bring you The Adventures of Nick Train: Spy-Hunter. Ohio Bars are famed the world around for their rich chocolaty coating and their delicious nuts 'n 'nougat filling. You can't beat an Ohio Bar for a quick pick-me-up when you feel the need for an energy burst, or for the sheer eatin' pleasure of finest Brazilian chocolate, nuts'n'nougat from around the world. Especially in wartime, yes, now more than ever, you can't afford to pass up the day's best bargain, a five-cent chocolate Ohio Bar.

Dayton stopped the tape and swung around in his chair. 'Bet you never heard of Ohio Bars. They don't make 'em anymore. Used to be a lot of regional candy bars; everything got gobbled up by national brands. I like to drop these period commercials into my shows, especially for products nobody knows about. Ohio Bars are a special favorite because of my name.' He looked at her expectantly. After a beat he said, 'Ohio Bars. Lon Dayton. Dayton, Ohio. See?'

Marvia managed a feeble smile. Dayton was wearing a pair of whipcord bell-bottoms and a polyester print shirt with pictures of Andy Panda all over it. She gave him her name and ran her Robert Bjorner spiel, adding Sun Mbolo's name to the list. Dayton brightened and shook her hand.

'Could I get you away from your work for a little while, Mr. Dayton? Or would you rather finish up before we talk?'

He said he was almost finished. She nodded and he turned back to the editing machine, where he performed another razor-blade-and-adhesive operation and hit the rewind button. A few seconds later he lifted the tape from the deck and closed it in a box. 'Tonight's show. I don't like to work too far ahead. I think it takes the edge off my sharpness, don't you?' He stood up. 'Now, I must say it took you a while to get to me. I don't suppose you're questioning sources in ascending order of importance, by any chance? Because that would explain why you didn't come sooner. Could I see your credentials, by the way? Not that I doubt your bona fides, but a person in my position can't be too careful.'

She showed him her badge again.

'Seems real enough. Anything else?'

She sighed and handed him a business card.

He held it up to the light, extracted a card case from a pocket in his whipcord bells, and offered his own card in exchange. It was laminated, with a hologram of the KRED red radio logo on one side. When Marvia moved the card under the ceiling light, electrical bolts zapped out of the radio.

'Very impressive.' She turned the card over. It had Dayton's name on it, along with the slogan 'King of Old-Time Radio', and the Barbara Jordan Boulevard address. She slipped it into her pocket. 'No home address,' she commented.

'I choose to keep my personal life separate from my professional activities.'

'But you do live at the McGee location?'

'I maintain a pied-à-terre on McGee. Mainly for my archives.'

'Where do you live?'

'When I'm in Berkeley I do use the McGee suite. Otherwise, well, where my work takes me, there I go.' He grinned at her. He looked like a dog pulling its lips back from its clenched teeth in a desperate effort to please its master. 'Did you hear any of that tape I was working on, Sergeant Plum?'

'Just the commercial. I think I heard part of a Nick Train show the other morning.'

'Yes, yes. Last-minute cancellation. *The Wax Mine*. Disc jockey didn't show up for work. I got a panic phone call and ran in with a Nick Train I've been cleaning up. One of my favorite series. And if I were to tell you what I know about Nick Train, you'd be very, very surprised. A word to the wise, eh?' He laid a finger against the side of his nose and winked.

'Is this a good time to talk about Robert Bjorner and Sun Mbolo?' Marvia asked.

'Good time.' Dayton lowered his voice. 'Wrong place. Do you have a secure facility at the Hall of Justice, Sergeant? Or — better yet!' He actually seemed to have surprised himself. 'I could admit you to the McGee facility. With precautions, of course. Are you armed?'

'That's not something I discuss.'

'Oh, I understand. You're in mufti today, as we say in the — well, as we say. Come along, I'll drop off the tape in 'up for play' in case I don't make it back to the studio in time.' He stopped at the receptionist's desk and told Jessie Loman to hold all his calls, please, indefinitely. He jerked his head toward Marvia. Jessie nodded.

On the sidewalk he said, 'I didn't bring my own conveyance today. Do you think we could ride in your cruiser?'

Marvia said, 'Sure.' She opened the passenger-side door of the black-and-white, and Dayton climbed in with the expression of a high-school kid getting his first ride in a hot rod.

She circled the car and climbed in, checked her on-board computer and found three messages. One was from Patrol. They'd checked with city hall and learned that Mbolo had rented her house from a retired UC prof who had moved to Bhutan to research variations in Buddhist scriptural texts. No known next of kin. Emergency contact was Parlie Sloat, c/o Oceana Foundation.

The second was from the front desk. The brainstorming session was set for Monday at ten a.m., patrol briefing room. She had two days and three nights to prepare. Normally that would be plenty of time, but this case had started out complicated enough, and became recomplicated with the second killing.

The third message was from Gemma

Silver at the coroner's office. Autopsy on Sun Mbolo was set for the next morning at eight. Swell. Marvia would have to leave Jamie in the house, grounded, and head off to Oakland alone for the happy event.

She drove Dayton to McGee and parked. He lived in a stucco-covered four-story building that had last been renovated, she estimated, during Dwight Eisenhower's first term.

Dayton led the way up creaking stairs. His suite was a single room. There was a sink in the corner, and a miniature refrigerator. A battered mattress lay on the floor, a filthy sleeping bag on top of it. The walls were decorated with posters advertising radio shows of the 1940s. There was an elaborate audio system and an editing deck similar to the one Dayton had used at KRED. A grimy window looked out into McGee Avenue.

'So you're an admirer of Nick Train's?' he asked.

Marvia wasn't pleased with the way this contact was going. But maybe she'd let him run for a while, then rein him in if he didn't give her anything useful.

'I've just heard a little.'

'The spy-hunter series was just the wartime stuff, you know. Before the war Nick was a crime-buster. And after the war he got into commie-smashing. That's been a problem at KRED. They're all soft on communism. Really soft. I mean, you wave a copy of *Das Kapital* in there and everybody salutes. You know?'

'I thought the station was changing its programming philosophy.'

'Well, some. That's why I like to stick in those old commercials, just to tweak some of their tail feathers. Ohio Bars. Ha! Krunch-Rite, Huron & Erie Radiators. Hah! At first they wouldn't let me use 'em. We finally compromised — I can only run commercials for products that don't exist anymore.'

Then he got somber. 'I don't know, now that Sun Mbolo's gone. Word is, they're sending somebody down from Oceana. Maybe Parlie Sloat. She used to run KRED before Zelman left Oceana, then she moved up there. But I think she's coming back to run KRED, at least for a while. Weird woman. Never liked her. I think she's part of the group. Look!' He held up his hands and made an odd gesture. What was it, some kind of lodge recognition sign?

When Marvia failed to respond, he looked disappointed. 'I'm going to let you in on a secret,' he said. 'Lot of people think Nick Train was a fictitious character. He wasn't. I mean — which episode did you hear?'

'Something about a princess in Oaxaca and an airplane, a Super Bomber.'

'Good, good!' Dayton's eyes were gleaming. 'That was a true story, you know. It's still classified, but some of us know about it and we're using the airwaves to get the word out to the struggling masses, you see?'

Marvia said, 'I'm afraid I don't.' She looked around the room. There was a rickety wooden chair in front of the editing deck.

Dayton caught her eye movement. 'Want to have a seat, Sergeant? We have a lot to discuss. What time is it?' He looked at his wristwatch. It was a massive black

268

thing not much smaller than a hockey puck, with knobs and buttons all around its rim. 'Huh, seventeen forty-eight hours. Good. I trust you don't have an urgent appointment.'

She waited.

'Of course his name wasn't Nicholas Train, and all of the other characters' names had to be disguised as well. And the Electro Super Bomber — well, did you ever hear of the XB-200? No, of course not. It was one of Uncle Sam's best-guarded secrets. One of the greatest secrets of the twentieth century, in fact. It — '

'*Mr. Dayton!*' Marvia had had enough. 'What can you tell me either about Robert Bjorner or Sun Mbolo?'

'I think they were part of the group. I think the other side got to them, and I'll probably be next.'

'What group?' Marvia asked. 'What other side?'

Dayton made his gesture again. He looked at one hand. 'Atlantis,' he whispered. And at the other. 'Lemuria.' He looked up at Marvia. 'It was inevitable. Couldn't prevent it. Some of us tried, tried very hard, but it had to come. Had to. Even Train couldn't stop it. You want to know Nicholas Train's real name, Sergeant, do you?'

Marvia said, 'Sure.'

'Lon Dayton!' He beamed. 'We all had secret identities. The Shadow was Lamont Cranston, except when he was Kent Allard. The Spider was Richard Wentworth. Captain Midnight, the Green Lama, the Mysterious Traveler, even Superman. I'll bet you didn't know that the Blue Beetle was really Dan Garrett before Dr. Franz gave him Vitamin X-2. He was a police officer. Maybe you knew him. Did you ever meet Officer Garrett?'

'No, I'm afraid I never met Officer Garrett.'

'Well, don't let that impostor tell you he's Blue Beetle. He isn't. Dan Garrett is.'

'What impostor?'

'Steve Insetta. He's no Blue Beetle. He's no superhero. He's a phony.'

Marvia's heart sank.

17

Marvia sat at her old schoolgirl desk in her old room. Maybe she'd better get a head start on the brainstorming session. The more she thought about it, the more she realized that one night's preparation would be insufficient.

She pulled open a drawer and found a yellow pad. She thought back just a few hours to her interview with Lon Dayton. When he'd exploded his bombshell about Steve Insetta, she had felt the world drop out from under her feet. She'd been ready to dismiss Dayton as a harmless eccentric. Herb Bjorner's description of the typical KRED hanger-on had fit him to a T. His talk about secret conspiracies and super-bombers and ancient radio dramas based on reality was irrational, sure, but as long as he didn't harm anybody, who cared? There were enough crazies in Berkeley to fill a stadium, and nobody bothered to do much about them.

Certainly it wasn't Marvia's job to play mental health worker. But when Dayton mentioned Blue Beetle and used the name Steve Insetta, he wasn't just a harmless eccentric anymore. He became still another connecting strand in a complex spiderweb of personalities and events.

'What do you know about Steve Insetta?' Marvia had asked.

'He hangs around sometimes. You know, the station gets pretty deserted late at night. We lock up the street doors. People come in and do their shows and go home.'

Marvia had learned early on about KRED's somewhat feeble security system. The keypads mounted outside the station's front and rear doors would never stop a professional cracksman, or even a clever hacker with enough energy to leave his computer for ten minutes.

She asked Dayton, 'Do you have a personal door-code?'

'Sure. Every time they decide too many people are wandering in and out of the station they give out a whole new set.'

'Steve Insetta doesn't have a code, does he?'

Dayton shrugged. 'He's an old KRED hand. I never gave him my code but he always manages to get one. He wanders in sometimes when I'm in the studio. We just bullshit a little. Sometimes he brings his squeeze with him.'

'Alice?'

'Alice, yeah. I don't know who she is.'

'What do you mean? You don't know her last name?'

Dayton smiled. 'I'm awfully hungry. You think we could go out for some grub? I can tell you some more, but I really need my supper.'

Marvia closed her eyes. It was getting late; she wanted to check in her police cruiser and shower up and go home. She wanted to see Jamie. More, she wanted Jamie to see her.

'You want a snack?' she asked Dayton. 'How about, huh, you know Shaughnessy's?'

Dayton brightened. 'Sure. Right around the corner from KRED. Let's do it!'

En route to the restaurant, Dayton

informed her that he sometimes used Shaughnessy's for secret rendezvous with his confidential contacts. If he was seen dining there with Sergeant Plum it might prove beneficial to her work.

As they entered the restaurant Marvia came face to face with Maude Markham. The reporter did a double take, said hello to Marvia and to Dayton, and kept rolling. Marvia could imagine the rumors flying around KRED after *that* little encounter.

She sat down opposite Dayton. What the hell was she doing pondering the menu chalked on a blackboard behind the bar in a musty Irish saloon, sitting opposite a certifiable wacko, when she should be home with her son?

Dayton ordered a huge meal. Obviously he expected Marvia to pick up the tab, and she resigned herself to doing so. It was still possible that Dayton would have something good for her. He'd already given her another link between Steve Insetta and KRED. For herself, she ordered only a cup of vegetable soup and a grilled cheese sandwich. Lon Dayton seemed unfamiliar with such exotic implements as a knife and fork. Marvia sipped tea from a heavy restaurant cup with her meal. The place was fairly full; far more customers seemed interested in alcohol than in dinner. Dayton attacked his food ferociously. Marvia suspected that this was indeed his first meal of the day, maybe of the past couple of days. When he slowed down a little she put a question to him.

'Who else has the night code for KRED besides you? Not everybody who works at the station, do they?' There was a chance here of tracking the entry code from Insetta back to its source inside the station. If she could do that . . .

'Lots of people.' Dayton didn't stop chewing to answer. 'Engineering staff. Jem Waller and them. All the late programmers. Margarita. Bix.'

'Margarita and Bix? How often did you see them?'

'They came in to do their shows. Margarita lives up in Richmond. Her partner always brings her. She uses that van, you know, with the wheelchair lift on it. Susan what's-her-face, she drives Margarita and helps her with everything.'

'And Beiderbecke?'

'You know, he lives right next to the station. In the back of his store.'

'Let's get back to Steve Insetta.'

'The Blue Beetle.' Dayton grinned. 'I knew all along that Officer Garrett business was a dodge. Once I met Steve, I knew right away what was going on.'

'Did you ever see them together?' *Come on, you Looney Tune, focus!*

'You mean, like, Margarita and Susan and Bix and Steve and Alice?'

'That's exactly what I mean.'

'No, not all at once. Steve used to come in sometimes and hang out. Him and Alice. They used to deal to half the staff.'

'Did you ever buy drugs from Insetta?'

Dayton giggled. 'I never had any. I thought of making some illicit buys to get a line on what was going on, but my agency budget would never cover it so I merely observed. But I knew there was nothing to worry about. I mean, the Beetle must have been on to something really big. Really, *really* big. You know? I used to slip him the high sign and he always knew the order of the day. Good man. Valuable to the agency.'

'What did he sell, Mr. Dayton?'

'Everything. He'd make the deal, Alice would deliver the goods. Pot, 'shrooms, ice, crack, plain blow. You name it. Thai stick. Paraphernalia.'

Dayton knew the language, then. But did he know what he was talking about, or was he just mouthing off, trying to make an impression?

'What paraphernalia?' Marvia asked. 'Drug paraphernalia?'

He nodded. 'Sometimes lethal force is needed, Sergeant Plum. Or should I say, Agent Plum? Or is that your name at all?' He looked like a true believer who had died and found himself in heaven.

'Please be specific. Handguns? Assault weapons? Explosives?'

'Whatever our people need, Agent, it's our job to see to it that they get. Right?'

'Did Insetta supply drugs to Robert Bjorner? Do you know if they ever had contact?'

'Radio Red was a day guy. Agent

Garrett — ' He snickered. ' — only came in at night. Bjorner would have had to make his pickups at the Wax Cylinder, but that was no problem. Bix and Beetle and Alice used to be a triad. They were water brothers, you know. On Mars, Agent Plum. They go that far back.'

Marvia thanked him. Shaughnessy's was getting more jammed by the minute. 'Can you get home yourself, Mr. Dayton?'

Dayton darted a glance at Huntington Way. The black-and-white stood at the curb across the street from Shaughnessy's. There were a few other parked cars and a scattering of vehicles passing through puddles of light from the streetlamps. Foot traffic seemingly had ended for the night.

'Frankly, Agent, now that we've been seen together you know, I left my op center unarmed. My mistake, counter to agency policy, I know. But I can usually rely on my fists alone.'

Marvia drove him back to his apartment, then sat outside in the cruiser rubbing her eyes. She ought to pack it in, go home, spend some time with Jamie, and get a decent night's rest for once. But she wasn't ready for that. She was getting greedy for facts. One more fact and one more fact and one more connection and . . . a case would be solved! She'd done it before and she wanted to do it again. A rush came with it.

She drove back to Barbara Jordan Boulevard and revisited Bara Miyako. She'd arranged earlier to chat with Miss Kato and the chef, Mr. Hiroshi Kojima, and this was the time to do it.

In the meantime she decided she'd found an exception to the rule that everybody lied to cops. She was convinced that Lon Dayton was absolutely sincere in every word that he spoke. Absolutely sincere and absolutely crazy. There was no telling how much reality lay behind his stories of Leon Beiderbecke and the team of Insetta and Gonser dealing drugs and weapons to KRED staffers, but she suspected there was at least a grain of truth in the story. And if there was, then her web of fine strands was becoming ever more dense and drawing ever tighter around KRED. But first she needed to talk with Kato and Kojima.

Kato couldn't have been more than nineteen. She stood taller than most Japanese. Her hair was blue-black and glossy, hanging from an elaborately carved shell at the peak of her head. She said, 'I'll help you any way I can, Sergeant. What do you want?'

She knew Robert Bjorner from his frequent visits to the restaurant. She didn't know anything about him; she never listened to KRED. And she had no idea who Sun Mbolo was, or had been. She did her work, waiting tables at Bara Miyako and shopping for supplies at the Okutaro Hanto fish and poultry market on San Pablo Avenue. She carried a full course load at UC. And she modeled clothing in her spare time for the *Examiner* Sunday magazine.

'They like me because I have long bones and an Asian face. They think I'm exotic and clothes look good on me. Once I get my degree, that's that — I'm out of here and I'm out of modeling.' She was going to be a physicist.

None of that was particularly useful, and none of it was the real surprise. The surprise was that she was the grand-daughter of the chef, Hiroshi Kojima. 'My parents came to the States in '72. I was born here, of course. My dad was an orphan. Mr. Kojima is my mom's dad. When Grandma died, Mom and Dad went back to Japan and brought him over here. They live in Seattle, but the Fujis are our cousins and I'm living with them while I study at Cal. They needed a chef for the restaurant, and my grandpa is a great chef. But he doesn't know any English. I'll translate for you, if you want to talk with him.' Marvia did indeed want to talk with Mr. Kojima.

He was another surprise. Yaeko Kato went to the kitchen to fetch him, and when they returned she trailed one hand behind her. He reached forward, his fingers barely touching her hand, and maneuvered through the tables.

Marvia stood up. Kojima bowed. His face was a mask of scar tissue. Marvia said, 'Please, let's all sit down.'

Yaeko Kato spoke in Japanese and Kojima nodded, locating a chair. The case involved a nearly blind broadcaster, a blind computer programmer, and now a blind chef.

With Kato's help, Marvia went through her litany of questions. Kojima held his head cocked, listening as Marvia asked each question. Then he turned his head to follow his granddaughter's translation. After each question he grunted his answers to Kato, who translated them for Marvia.

He didn't know Bjorner or Mbolo. He didn't listen to the radio. He wasn't even aware that Bara Miyako was located next to a radio station. He did his work. He was proud of his ability. He could run the kitchen without seeing anything. Yes, he had been a chef all his life. He was seventy-four years old, and as strong as a young man. He had been a chef all his life. He had been a chef for the Imperial Marines in World War Two, and been terribly burned by white phosphorus on Tarawa in 1943. He would not have been captured, but he was blinded and helpless and could find no weapon with which to fight the enemy or take his own life.

Fugu? Pufferfish?

If he had his eyes, he would have learned the art and received his license in Japan. But even the great Hiroshi Kojima could not make *fugu* without seeing what he was doing.

The day of Bjorner's death? At work, of course.

The night of Mbolo's death? At work, still.

He had a few cronies; they met and drank sake and talked in Japantown in San Francisco — his daughter took him there by train and bus every now and then. But mainly he worked and rested. At his age, and blind, there was little else to do.

Marvia thanked him. He stood up and said a few more words. Yaeko Kato translated them. He offered his respects to the noble police officer, and he was going back to work scrubbing out his kitchen and preparing for the next day's tasks.

Marvia stood outside the Bara Miyako.

There was mist in the air and the streetlamps were haloed.

Radio Red had died of poisonous Japanese food out of a Bara Miyako carton. He'd served with the United States Marines and been blinded on Tarawa. Hiroshi Kojima was the chef at Bara Miyako, and he had served with the Japanese Imperial Marines and been blinded on Tarawa. It seemed too good to be true. Had Kojima borne a grudge for more than fifty years, and decided to get revenge against Bjorner? Kojima denied knowing Bjorner or even knowing anything about KRED, but everyone lied to the cops, even honest citizens. Surely a murderer was not to be trusted.

She strolled past the KRED/Oceana building, toward Huntington Way.

The biggest question was how the Bjorner and Mbolo killings were connected. It was possible, just possible, that they weren't. What if Hiroshi Kojima had killed Bjorner out of long-simmering resentment dating back to World War Two . . . and Insetta had killed Mbolo, with or without the help of Alice Gonser, for some as-yet unclear reason having to do with Solomon San Remo and their drug-dealing activities and the internal politics of KRED? What if, she realized, these were actually two different cases that she had been deceived into thinking were one?

A ragged form stepped around the corner from Huntington Way. Marvia froze. It was Maude Markham again.

'Say, how was your meal? I'm new in town and I could still give you a better steer than Shaughnessy's for a cozy dinner for two.'

Marvia looked into the older woman's eyes. 'Do you just wander the streets all night, Maude?'

Markham smiled. 'You meet the most interesting people that way.' She leaned toward Marvia. 'You getting anywhere on the murders? Lot of people are spooked at KRED, you know.'

Marvia shook her head. 'Nothing to tell you, Maude.'

'My, my. Sounds grim to me.'

Marvia said, 'It may take a while, but we'll solve it. You can bet on it.'

18

'Hey, my big sis, what are you doin'? That's no place to sleep.'

Marvia opened her eyes, turned slowly and smiled. 'Tyrone.' She was still half-asleep. She was wearing a plaid long-sleeved shirt and jeans, and she'd been working on her notes for the brainstorming session. 'What time is it?'

'One thirty.'

'Tyrone!' She slid her chair back from the desk and pushed herself to her feet. Her arm gave way and she caught herself with her other hand. She had fallen asleep with her head on one arm, and with the circulation cut off she felt only a weak tingling from the elbow down. She peered at the window. Darkness.

'I was driving by and thought I'd drop in, see if you were still up. Actually I thought you'd be in bed, but I saw some lights.'

'I was working. I just put my head

same. Did you hear what happened to Tanya Johnson? She was shooting meth and she got AIDS from a dirty needle. I don't know which is worse, to spend years with it and then die or to die fast.'

'Yeah. She was always a frail little thing. I guess she didn't have much in reserve.' He picked up his Modelo Negra and rolled the label against his cheek. 'Little Jamie kind of left that part out.'

'Did he tell you about K'neesha Baldwin?'

'I know that family. They moved up north. So what?'

'Did he mention the guns? Did he mention a pair of dealers called Blue Beetle and Acid Alice?'

'Kind of. Jamie told me you asked him to go underground for the narcs. You gonna put your own son out there? You think that's fair? What's his dad have to say about it?'

'It's up to Inspector Stillman. We haven't made up our minds. And we'll probably get somebody in from Youth Bureau and an assistant DA. But I think we've found another way around that. I think Jamie and his pal Hakeem will sign statements for Stillman, and once that happens they can fade out of the case. And we caught another break, too.'

'Yeah? What?'

'We busted a guy and he's willing to snitch 'em out to save himself.'

Tyrone nodded.

'As for Jamie, he holds Beetle and Alice responsible for Tanya's death and K'neesha's troubles. The Baldwins didn't just move away, Tyrone, they got out of town to save their daughter. Jamie knew those girls and now he wants to get back at Beetle and Alice.'

Tyrone nodded. 'Maybe Jamie ought to spend some time with his papa, whether ol' Wilkerson likes it or not. I don't see how he can say no to that, big sis.'

Marvia said nothing.

'That's not what you wanted to hear, is it?'

She shook her head.

'Sometimes you gotta hear what you don't wanna hear. Papa used to say that, you remember?'

She whispered, 'Yes. I don't want to

send him away, but I'll do it if I must. But you don't know Jamie's dad the way I do, or that witch of a new wife of his, Claudia the ice queen. If I send them Jamie, they might never send him back.'

Tyrone shrugged. 'Up to you, sister. What's your choice?'

'Get rid of the creeps in the park. I don't think Jamie would get involved again. I think he's on the road to Damascus, Tyrone. He's got to make a decision. It isn't fair, he's still a little boy, but he's still got to make a decision.'

'You think he'll make the right choice?'

'I'll never forgive myself if I'm wrong, Tyrone.'

He tilted his Modelo Negra. It was empty. 'I think I better get rolling. I got a Gremlin comin' into the shop. You believe that? Some nutty millionaire bought himself a damned AMC Gremlin and he wants me to restore it to like-new. Well, ours not to reason why, is it, big sister?'

She managed a small smile.

A few hours and coffees later, she managed to wake up enough to head into Oakland for the Mbolo autopsy. Edgar

Bisonte presided, but his protégé and heir apparent, Leo Golden, M.D., did most of the slicing. Marvia suited up in medical greens and stood alongside Sun Mbolo's replacement as general manager of KRED, Parlie Sloat.

They'd assembled beforehand in Bisonte's office. Parlie Sloat introduced herself and offered Marvia a warm handshake. She was tall and broad-shouldered, with wavy blond hair and blue eyes and the kind of complexion white girls were supposed to want. 'I was shocked when I heard about Tamar,' she said. 'You know, I held that job before she did. When Sid Zelman retired from Oceana and I moved up, I brought her in and gave her the chance to run the station.

'At first, Mr. Bisonte was reluctant to let me attend this function. Family and concerned public officials only. But I told him I *am* Tamar's family. There's no one else. I'm the closest thing. And he said, 'Well, all right, then,' so here I am.'

No one had used the name Tamar Tasira in this case before. Mbolo had been unwilling to use it even at KRED. But Parlie Sloat used it and it probably didn't matter. Surely the Dirgue couldn't harm Mbolo any more.

'Ms. Sloat, how did you know that name?' Marvia asked.

'Tamar? But, Sergeant, I helped her get her start in America. I was her guide. I brought her into KRED and I helped her along.'

Marvia studied the bigger woman. She spoke with the soft tone of white southern aristocracy. Yet she was running a network of radio stations whose politics were anywhere from ultraliberal to revolutionary, and taking a black African Jewish woman under her wing and helping her climb the ladder.

'And now I'm back in the KRED office, at least for a while. There was so much infighting at KRED, I just had to step in myself. There was no other way.'

That was when they'd been summoned to the autopsy room. Marvia wondered if Parlie Sloat knew what she was in for.

Golden had a pompous mien and a

voice that sounded as if he'd been trained for the stage. 'The remains before us are those of a mature African female between the ages of thirty-five and forty. Her demise would appear to be the result of a deep incision to the lower back, performed with a sharp instrument penetrating the epidermis and incising the internal organs, causing death by exsanguination. We will determine whether this is in fact the case, and ask and answer many other questions, including that of possible rape or sexual assault.' Beside Marvia, Parlie Sloat shuddered.

Dr. Golden completed the gross external examination of the body, noting that it was largely intact and undamaged except for the major wound in the lower back and the numerous puncture wounds to the chest. He noted that there were seventeen of these, fourteen to the left chest and breast, three to the right. The angle of the wounds indicated a thin sharply pointed object entering from the victim's left and from a slightly elevated position.

Marvia followed closely. Golden's

descriptions of the wounds were those of a medical man. Her understanding was that of a homicide detective: the assailant had been right-handed and had been taller — but not much taller — than his victim.

Before incising the cadaver, Golden had it turned to a prone position. He described the major wound as to its width, approximately 8 centimeters, and its height, approximately 0.5 centimeters at its right terminus and narrowing in a triangular wedge shape toward the left. Entry was above the right pelvic bone, the blade moving toward the victim's left and severing the spinal cord.

Marvia converted the measurements in her mind. The wound was a little more than 3 inches wide and 0.2 inches high, at the right end. Again, the wound would have been inflicted by an attacker surprising his victim. A right-handed individual, his forearm level with his waist, holding a knife in the most common manner, point forward and sharpened edge to the left.

Marvia compared Golden's figures to

her examination of the blackened implements she'd seen in the fireplace at Sun Mbolo's house. The evidence techs had those now, and they would be working on them, though once the flames had done their work there was little chance of any usable matter remaining on the kitchen knife or the ice-pick. Still, the dimensions were a good fit. There was little doubt that Mbolo's attacker had used the kitchen knife to kill her and the ice-pick to inflict the postmortem punctures.

Was Steve Insetta right- or left-handed?

An anal examination and swab indicated slight irritation but no presence of other foreign substances. Golden had the cadaver returned to a supine position. A vaginal examination detected signs of possible battering and slight tearing, but a swab yielded no evidence of recent intercourse. Straightening, Golden moved to the head of the cadaver and performed an oral swab to determine the presence of foreign substances, without positive results.

'We will now proceed to an examination of the internal organs.'

That was when Parlie Sloat toppled over. Although she was six inches taller than Marvia Plum and outweighed her easily by thirty pounds, Marvia was able to catch her and lower her to the floor without injury. Golden did not look up from his work. An orderly and a security guard loaded Sloat onto a gurney and removed her from the autopsy room.

Marvia had learned what she needed from the autopsy. If there were any surprises, she was certain she'd get them from Leo Golden. In the meanwhile, she had already invited him to Monday's brainstorming session, along with Gemma Silver.

Parlie Sloat moaned and stirred, then sat up, trembling. Her peaches-and-cream complexion had turned a pallid gray. She focused on Marvia and held out a hand.

Marvia caught it and said, 'You had a little fainting spell. Happens to almost everybody the first time.'

Sloat gazed around the room, then down at the gurney. 'Yow, get me off this thing.'

Marvia helped her off the gurney.

'Think you want to sit down for a few minutes, or would you rather get some fresh air?'

'Let's get out of here.'

Once they were outside, Sloat started west on Fourth Street. Marvia kept pace despite Sloat's longer legs. She said, 'I think we need to talk, Ms. Sloat.' When that failed to draw a response, Marvia placed her hand on the bigger woman's wrist.

'I'm really very shaken, Sergeant. I've never seen such a vile and even filthy performance as that Dr. Golden's.'

'It's standard practice. Look, suppose there had been sperm on the cadaver. If we have a suspect, we could look for a DNA match and either rule him out or start building our case against him.'

Sloat shuddered visibly; theatrically in fact, Marvia thought. 'Surely there is a less . . . demeaning way.'

'Dr. Golden didn't demean Sun Mbolo. Whoever murdered her demeaned her. We have to use every tool at our disposal to find that killer. The coroner will check for skin under her fingernails, blood, saliva, urine, feces, anything he can find. We need it all. Now don't you go all queasy and coy on us when this investigation is — maybe — finally getting somewhere.' She had Sloat's attention now, and she wasn't ready to let it go. 'Just from what we saw in there, we know some things about the killer that we didn't know before. And we have some puzzling facts, too. If — '

She stopped herself. What she had to say didn't belong in a conversation with this person. It belonged in tomorrow's brainstorming session.

Marvia saved the rest.

19

She got Wilma Ransome's home number from the UC police and called her. The Tuesday-through-Friday Radio Red scripts had been converted from Braille to type and were ready to pick up, but Ransome would have to open the secure file cabinet for her.

Marvia dropped off the Mustang at the Hall of Justice and drove a black-and-white to Ransome's home. They rode together to the UC computer sciences building. Ransome was as good as her word. Marvia asked again if she had read any of the material, and Ransome repeated that she had checked the Braille scripts purely for reference. Her computer lash-up included a voder, and she could play back Bob Bjorner's scripts in a voice, but it wouldn't be Bjorner's voice and it wouldn't have the inflection that he would have given the material.

After dropping Ransome off, Marvia

turned Bjorner's Braille scripts over to the evidence room and carried the printouts to her desk. She found a message from Agent Nicholas Train.

Oh, boy. *Nick Train: Spy-Hunter*. It had to be Lon Dayton, the King of OTR and all the rest of that malarkey. This was all she needed. Would Agent Plum contact Agent Train using secure channels on a matter of the utmost importance and sensitivity? She punched in his McGee number and asked what he had for her.

'Are you sure this is a secure line, Agent?'

'Absolutely.'

'I still think a face-to-face contact is indicated.'

'You don't want to tell me what you have there?'

'It isn't that, Agent. I don't . . . dare. As risky as it would be for me, the real issue is your own safety and well-being.'

Right. The guy was a nutcase. But somewhere in that twisted mind there lurked something important to this case.

Marvia locked the Bjorner scripts in

her desk and drove to Dayton's apartment. He greeted her at the door, peering up and down the stale-smelling corridor to make sure no one was lurking. He was wearing the same polyester shirt and stained bell-bottoms he'd worn at their previous meeting. He hadn't shaved or, apparently, washed his face or his hands.

'I told you I have a major archive of broadcast materials,' he said. 'I didn't tell you that it includes a treasure trove of KRED history. I've been tracking it down for years, finding people who had old ETs, home recordings, tapes, anything. You'd be surprised how many Berkeleyans have followed KRED over years and have files of shows and program guides in their homes.'

'Your point is?'

'Did you know that the inaugural broadcast of KRED was preserved on seventy-eight RPM discs? They were offered as premiums for new members. That was back in the days of free red radios. People who already had FM radios could get seventy-eight RPM discs. They had a band playing, and Kingston,

Rosemere, Eisenberg and D'Allessandro all made speeches. They had the Mayor of Berkeley and the Chancellor of the University of California. KRED was going to be an integral member of the Berkeley community.'

'What does this have to do with the two killings?' Marvia snapped.

Dayton drew back, then smiled as if he'd just got a grand inside joke. 'I understand — Agent.'

He took two quick strides, all there was room for, and reached to his greatest height. Then he ran his finger down a huge vertical column of cassette boxes. 'KRED, all of it. I have the first debate that KRED sponsored between the supporters and critics of the International Scientific Sanity Society. I have — all right, I can see you're getting impatient. All right.' He whirled dramatically. 'I have the very first Radio Red show.'

She waited for him to continue.

'I have Radio Red and the big tax scandal. Right here.' He pulled a Lucite cassette case from the stack and held it in the air. 'This is Red's big exposé — the one that almost got him kicked off the air, but the old Berkeley *Gazette* got into the act and they didn't dare.' He tilted his head. 'Do you remember the Berkeley *Gazette*?'

Marvia admitted that she did.

'Did you know that Bob Bjorner went on the air the first year KRED was broadcasting? That was 1948. You'll find his inaugural broadcast fascinating. He was ready to expose Harry Truman as a crypto-fascist and show how the Marshall Plan was just a ploy by American imperialists to extend capitalist hegemony across the continent of Europe. And then when he got onto the Baruch Plan — do you remember the Baruch Plan, Agent?'

Marvia murmured, 'No.'

'Course not. Long before your time. Well, never mind, that's all over now.'

Marvia dodged the mattress and sleeping bag that passed for Lon Dayton's bed and tried to open the room's sole window. It wouldn't budge. Painted shut, who could guess how many decades ago.

'That's a security measure,' Dayton explained from behind her.

'All right. What about this supposed tax issue?'

'Did you know that Radio Red was coming up on fifty years at KRED? He wanted to retire. He wanted to put in his fifty years and get his testimonial dinner and his gold watch and just fade away. The station was close to its own fiftieth anniversary, and they were planning all sorts of self-congratulatory events. They wouldn't let him, though. They were trying to squeeze him out instead. Just the kind of nasty thing they'd do, too.'

'I thought you liked KRED.'

'Bunch of thugs there. I only let them have my show because I can reach other agents this way. You know.' He winked at her. 'That's how we made contact, isn't it, you and I.'

Marvia said, 'As a matter of fact, we made contact because of the death of Robert Bjorner. But if you could let me have that tape, the one you say has the tax material on it, it might be useful.' She held out her hand.

'I can't part with the original, you understand. Agency archive! But I've dubbed a copy for you.' He handed her a Lucite case containing an audiocassette. 'When you open that, you'll even find a photocopy of the *Gazette* piece that saved Red's job.'

Marvia opened the box and removed the copied newspaper clipping. For now she skimmed it; there would be time to read it thoroughly back at the Hall of Justice. But there was indeed a scandal going on. It involved the then-new KRED building on Austen Street. Austen had been renamed following the death of Barbara Jordan.

The Berkeley *Gazette* described a raging confrontation at a city council meeting. Parlie Sloat's name was prominently mentioned, as was that of council member Sherry Hanson. So much for the high ideals and squeaky-clean morality of KRED's famous four founders. By the time of this dispute, decades had passed and generations of managers had come and gone at KRED, and only a few stubborn holdovers like Bob Bjorner could hark back to the station's original character.

Why was this all new to Marvia? She checked the dates on the cassette and the newspaper clipping. Well, she'd been in Wiesbaden at the time, defending the free world against the encroaching octopus of communist aggression. Her father had still been alive in those years, but neither her parents nor her brother had bothered to keep her posted on the controversy. Well, nothing surprising in that. She would hardly have cared anyway. They were busy keeping her posted on Tyrone's progress at Berkeley High.

So Lon Dayton had come through after all. Still another strand, actually a double one, connecting Parlie Sloat, Robert Bjorner, and Sherry Hanson. Of all people, Marvia Plum's longtime critic and arch nemesis, council member Sherry Hanson.

Lon Dayton, aka Agent Nicholas Train, didn't want a receipt for the cassette and photocopied news clipping. Didn't want to leave a paper trail that might fall into the hands of the wrong persons. Marvia left him in his secret base, picked up a takeout order from a taqueria on

University, drove back to McKinley Avenue, and ate at her desk.

She spread the transcripts of the final week of *Radio Red* shows on her desk. The first of them, Monday's planned broadcast, was the Khrushchev speech. All right, she knew all about that. For all that Ed Florio claimed that it was a disguised attack on Sun Mbolo, Marvia was hoping for something more overt.

On Tuesday, Bjorner turned elegiac. He didn't say anything about planning to retire, but he devoted his planned show to reviewing the history of the cold war. It was a remarkable performance, to cram forty-plus years of history into fifteen minutes. But Bjorner traced the struggle from the brief euphoria that followed the surrender of Germany and Japan to the Berlin blockade, the Marshall Plan, the Korean War, John Foster Dulles's concept of brinkmanship, Jacobo Arbenz Guzman, Zhou En-lai, and Patrice Lumumba. Some of the names Marvia remembered well. Others were only dimly and remotely familiar.

And Bjorner's ego shone through it all

when he spoke of the sacrifice he'd made for his country and the way his country had betrayed its great Soviet friends and supplied the imperialists with the means to break the backs of oppressed peoples. Oh, she'd heard this all before and was sick and tired of it.

Wednesday. 'My Famous Letter to Comrade Stalin.' Wow! This one was news. According to Bjorner, he had sat down and written a letter to Josef Stalin.

'On Stalin's birthday in 1949 I sent him a letter which I can say, in all modesty, almost certainly altered the course of history and saved our planet from total destruction. I quote:'

Iosif Vissarionovich! On the seventieth anniversary of your birth, I salute you in the name of working people and revolutionaries around the world. We see before us today, a mere four years after the destruction of the beast of fascism, the rise of new perils and tensions in all parts of the globe. The American ruling clique led by the political hack Truman, the Wall Street manipulator Acheson, and the madman Forrestal seek to turn back the inevitable rushing tide of history. Let them do so at their own peril. Future generations will know what to make of them. But for the present, dear Comrade, we must take care to avoid actions that will unleash forces of destruction . . .

Thursday. The tax thing. It wasn't obvious where Bjorner had got his data, but he must have had a mole in the city tax assessor's office. He referred back to the application process, and how KRED had managed to get away with an amazing break. The new building had replaced a decrepit theater. The old building, according to Bjorner's script, had been erected as the Jane Austen Playhouse at the corner of (then) Austen Street and Huntington Way shortly after 1900. It had started out offering high-class entertainment for the UC crowd, degenerated from a legitimate theater into a vaudeville house, then had fallen further to burlesque. At that point it was called, simply, Jane's.

When a reform administration in the 1940s had closed down burlesque in Berkeley, the theater switched to movies. The name was changed again, to the Austen. In the 1960s, in the face of heavy competition and shrinking audiences, the Austen gave up showing films and inaugurated a series of rock concerts. Business picked up for a while, but the theater developed a reputation for violence and drug-dealing and closed its doors for the last time in 1969. There it stood, vacant, until it was purchased by the Oceana Foundation, razed, and replaced by the new KRED/Oceana building.

Marvia furrowed her brow. What was scandalous about that? What had the Berkeley *Gazette* been so concerned about? She frowned, rubbed her eyes, then went back to Radio Red.

When Oceana bought the old theater from its previous owner, there was a huge tax obligation, long overdue. If the taxes had gone unpaid any longer, the city would surely have taken the building and the land it stood on, and auctioned them off. Instead, the property was sold to Oceana for a relative song. Something like half a million dollars, for a property that was potentially worth several times that, but where more than two million was owed in delinquent taxes. Something smelled rotten.

Council member Sherry Hanson was instrumental in setting up the whole deal, according to Bjorner. The general manager of KRED, who negotiated the deal from the radio station's side, was Parlie Sloat. And the former owner, who walked away with his pockets stuffed with money, was none other than Solomon San Remo.

Marvia had to get a drink of coffee. She brought it back to her desk, turned to Radio Red's Friday script, and read his farewell address:

A once noble institution, now corrupted and trivialized in the name of 'fun' and 'business,' an institution where half the staff spend half their time in various states of legal and illegal intoxication, an institution that has lost its heart and soul.

That was Radio Red's final opinion of

his beloved KRED, and that was why he was leaving the airwaves. So, Bjorner had decided to quit before he got fired. He'd given up the Golden Anniversary scheme, he was convinced that Sun Mbolo and the sellout gang were planning to pull the plug on his show, and he was determined to leave KRED under his own power before he got thrown out. Tragic.

The call from Dispatch hit Marvia like a bucket of ice water. It was a 187. Homicide. The address was a familiar number on McGee Avenue. Marvia's stomach churned. She jumped up, checked her S&W Airweight, and grabbed her jacket.

She knew better than to assume anything, but a cold sensation inside told her who the victim had to be. Lon Dayton, self-styled Agent Nick Train, had fallen in the line of duty. Just because you're paranoid doesn't mean you have no enemies. Dayton had enemies, and they'd got to him.

Marvia sprinted for the stairs.

★　★　★

It was easy enough to find the crime scene. Lon Dayton's professional-grade audio system was cranked to the max. A tape of an old cop show was playing, and McGee Avenue echoed with the screaming of police sirens, the chattering of tommy guns, and the shouts and moans of cops and crooks.

Abe Craigie had got to McGee Avenue already, and had a couple of patrol officers at work preserving the scene. Marvia made it up the creaking stairs almost as fast as she'd made it down the stairs at the Hall of Justice. She headed for Dayton's apartment and spotted Craigie at once. He smiled at her.

'No need, Marvia. Scene's under control.' He had to shout to make himself heard. He stepped over to the audio rig and studied it, then poked at the power switch with the tip of one latex-gloved finger. The sirens and tommy guns and voices went dead. The sudden silence struck with the impact of a blow to the solar plexus.

Marvia crossed the threshold and looked down at the cadaver, pulling on a pair of gloves of her own. The victim was Dayton, all right. Lon Dayton, the Lord of Laughter and Tears, was dead.

The musty odor of Dayton's one-room apartment was overridden by the odors of freshly spilled blood, freshly released body wastes, and fresh Japanese food. A carton bearing the Bara Miyako logo lay near the cadaver, its contents splattered on the bare floor, mixed with what had come out of Dayton. The body lay face down on the dirty wood.

Dayton was wearing the same ill-kept and outdated costume Marvia had seen during their previous meetings. His ridiculous bell-bottoms were pulled down around his thighs. There was no sign of underpants, but there was a long smear of blood close to each hip. There was a pattern of dark dots on his buttocks. A wooden handle that looked like that of an ice-pick stood upright between the cheeks. Marvia stifled a gasp and struggled to maintain her emotional distance. Without touching the cadaver, she took careful note that there were more punctures on the right buttock than the left. They resembled the ice-pick stabs that Sun Mbolo had suffered. Again, there was little blood around the ugly dark holes, suggesting that they had been inflicted after Dayton's death. He was barefoot.

Around him, the floor was littered with Lucite cassette boxes, thousands of them. Whoever had committed this crime had ransacked Dayton's precious tape archive; had turned the rows and columns of neatly tagged and filed programs into a hopeless hodgepodge. This time there was no fireplace. The killer had brought another wide-bladed kitchen knife and ice-pick with him. The disposition of the ice-pick was sickeningly clear. The knife, covered with blood, lay in the midst of the carnage. They would be checked for fingerprints, but this killer had used latex gloves at Sun Mbolo's house — assuming that it was the same killer — and he would have used them again at Dayton's apartment.

If she'd been called on to place a bet, Marvia would have given odds that Dayton's master tape of the Radio Red show dealing with the tax scandal over the old Austen Theater property would be missing — the cassette, the Lucite box that Dayton had stored it in, and the old Berkeley *Gazette* clipping that went with it. What the killer could not have known was that Dayton had turned over duplicates of both tape and clipping to Marvia.

'Abe, listen — I know this guy. You'll find my prints all over this place. I left here not two hours ago.'

Craigie pursed his lips and rolled his head on his shoulder. 'You think you should be here, Marvia?'

'What do you mean?'

'You just told me you knew the victim. You were here a couple of hours ago. You say you left your prints?'

'Yes, over there on the window. I tried to open it but it's painted shut.'

Craigie looked at the window. He was wearing latex gloves, but even so he didn't touch it. 'Nothing fishy going on here?' he asked.

'Totally on the up-and-up. Interview report is in the shop already.'

Craigie smiled. 'I should have known you'd do it right. Come on and have another look.'

318

20

By the time Marvia got home it was late, and she felt battered and exhausted. Jamie greeted her with the beginning of another diatribe about absent parents and broken promises, but when she actually began to cry he realized that he'd crossed a line. He backed off, then advanced again and took her hand and led her to a chair. She looked into his face and saw her father's eyes, somehow old and wise and patient.

He said, 'I'm sorry, Mom. Bad hair day?'

She laughed and grabbed his hand and kissed it. He took his hand back and stood there, embarrassed.

'We'll do something tomorrow, Jamie.'

'I'm grounded.'

'We'll sneak out. I'm trying to do better. Can you help me? What would you like to do? Do you need anything?'

'My mitt's pretty shabby. My hands have grown, you know. Look.'

She said, 'I know. How about a new mitt?'

'They're expensive.'

'We'll manage it. And we'll get our own place. Do you think you could live with an old lady like your mom? Just the two of us?'

'I could.' As he started to sniffle, he pulled a paper towel off the roll beside the sink and blew his nose into it.

'I'll start looking,' Marvia promised.

She glanced at the big battery-powered clock, then ran upstairs and phoned Dorothy Yamura and asked if they could make their dinner the following night instead.

★ ★ ★

The doorbell sounded and Marvia crossed the vestibule to answer it. Before she reached the door, she recognized Dorothy Yamura waiting on the veranda, standing beneath the overhead light. Her dark hair was cropped just below her ears and fluffed out to show her Asian features to their best advantage. She wore a heavy jacket and dark pants.

As Marvia opened the door Yamura said, 'Sorry I'm so late. Let's go eat.'

Marvia grabbed her own padded jacket and stepped onto the veranda.

Yamura asked, 'You have a place you want to go?'

'Any place out of Berkeley, or Oakland or Richmond. I don't want to run into anybody I know, and I especially don't want to hit any cop hangouts.'

Yamura grinned broadly. 'Got it.' She led the way to the curb and unlocked her car. It was a brand-new Buick. When Marvia slid into the soft leather seat and slammed her door, Yamura hit the ignition. The engine purred and soft music filled the car.

'Locatelli,' Yamura identified the music without being asked. '*The Art of the Violin*. My favorite. My daughter is learning these pieces.'

Marvia turned in her seat. 'I didn't know you had a daughter.'

'She lives with her grandparents in Pennsylvania.'

Yamura guided the Buick across

Berkeley and into the hills behind the old Claremont resort. In minutes the car was purring up a narrow road overhung by deciduous trees budding with new leaves. They dipped down into the town of Orinda and pulled into a paved parking lot. Yamura tossed the Buick's keys to a valet, and she and Marvia entered the restaurant.

It was like stepping into 1940. There was a huge bar backed with a polished mirror and white-jacketed bartenders wearing matching ties. The place was filled with Western regalia — murals, carvings, antique firearms. The bar was crowded, but Yamura found a pair of seats and she and Marvia slid onto them.

The shorter of the two bartenders nodded. 'Dorothy.'

Yamura said, 'George. This is my friend Marvia.'

George extended his hand. 'Pleasure. What can I get you?'

Marvia asked for a double bourbon on the rocks. Yamura raised an eyebrow.

George said, 'Usual, Dorothy?' She nodded.

George returned with their drinks and Yamura dropped a bill on the well-polished mahogany. She slid her shoulders out of her quilted jacket. Beneath it she wore an emerald silk blouse and a thin gold necklace. 'I never knew you drank bourbon,' she said to Marvia.

'I don't drink anything, much.' Marvia lifted her glass of whiskey, Yamura hers — a margarita — and they touched rims. Marvia slugged down a good swallow; the whiskey burned her throat and hit her stomach like a ball of flaming liquid.

Yamura took a small sip of her drink. 'So, why is tonight different from other nights?'

Marvia drew a breath. 'My life, Dorothy.' She wanted to tell her friend everything, but there was just too much of it.

Yamura tried again. 'You were with your friend Lindsey for — how long? Four, six years? — and all of a sudden he's gone and you're some other guy's blushing bride. I imagine that has to be part of it.'

Marvia nodded. 'I must be the world's worst judge of the male species, bar none.'

'You never met my ex.' Yamura grinned sourly.

'Yeah. Well, you knew the story of my stupid first marriage, to Lieutenant James Wilkerson.'

Yamura nodded. 'Now Congressman Wilkerson of the great state of Texas. I've seen him on TV.'

'When I got shot of Wilkerson I swore off men, and then I met Lindsey. All I needed was to get mixed up with a middle-aged white guy who lived with his crazed mother.'

George was back. 'Another?'

'Please,' Marvia replied.

The white-haired bartender flicked his eyes toward Dorothy Yamura. She nodded almost imperceptibly. Her margarita was less than half gone.

Marvia was feeling warmer now. She swung around on her stool and saw the reason: a huge stone fireplace with flaming logs in it. She hung her warm jacket, and Yamura's, on wooden pegs, then returned to her seat. Her glass was filled again. She vowed to make this drink last.

Yamura said, 'You have an appetite, Marvia?'

'Not yet.' She tasted her second bourbon. It was even better than the first.

'Didn't Lindsey's mother get better after a while?' Yamura asked. 'I thought you told me she was planning to remarry.'

'I think she did. I haven't been in touch with that family. Damn it, Dorothy, I shouldn't have thrown that guy back. I told myself I was dumping him for Jamie's sake — because he needed a black father, not a white one. But that wasn't the real reason. I was scared for me. Lindsey needed a real partner, you know, and I . . . my father died, you know, and I guess I felt lost and frightened. And who should turn up but Willie Fergus. Wonderful Willie. Here was this older guy who'd been like a father to me once before, so I married him. Mr. and Mrs. Willie Fergus.' She picked up her glass, then she put it down. 'That isn't the answer.'

Yamura said, 'Let's get food.'

They sat near the fireplace and Marvia felt the bourbon doing its work in her stomach. They ordered their meals, which were brought in short order.

'What went wrong with Mr. Fergus?' Yamura asked.

'I think the first morning we woke up together we realized we'd both made a mistake. I wanted a father, and he wanted a — I'm not sure. Maybe a French maid. You know, he really loved the bedroom part. I guess that was okay, but he didn't want to talk to me and he sure as hell didn't want me to talk to him. Not about anything real. Not about what I was thinking or what I wanted out of life.' She paused for a forkful of mashed potatoes. 'And he hated hearing me talk about Jamie. I guess I was feeling guilty about leaving Jamie with my mother; I wanted to talk about bringing him to live with us, and Willie wouldn't countenance that. Not a chance.'

Yamura made a sympathetic sound and Marvia kept rolling. 'He didn't care who I was as long as he got what he wanted. We tried to make it work, but it was impossible. I'm just glad that I got out of there and came back here. And thanks for getting me my job back, Dorothy. I know you had to go to the chief to get my stripes back for me. You went out on a limb and I appreciate it.'

'Okay, enough. Besides, that's shop, and we promised each other — '

The waitress asked if they wanted dessert. They both declined; Yamura asked for a cup of tea, Marvia for coffee.

On the way back to Berkeley, Yamura asked Marvia about her housing situation. Marvia explained how difficult it was. Yamura suggested that Marvia put a notice on the bulletin board at McKinley. Housing was perpetually tight in Berkeley, with the university community filling most of the available rental properties, but someone on the force might have a lead for her. You could never tell.

21

Marvia found herself facing a room full of people at the brainstorming session. She stood at the front of the briefing room, behind a table covered with notes and reports. A microphone stood on a lectern; its cord ran to a tape recorder. The reels were already revolving.

Lieutenant Yamura and Inspector Stillman sat side by side at the far end of the room, ready to listen but, as both had told Marvia before the session opened, less than eager to talk unless there were specific questions directed to them.

Just as Marvia had felt she was getting somewhere, the deaths of Mbolo and Dayton had added still another layer of confusion and cross-currents to the Bjorner case. Dayton had been the victim of another knife and ice-pick attack, and Marvia had every reason to believe that the same perp had been responsible for Mbolo's death.

A middle-aged African-American woman had taken a prominent seat in the front row of the briefing room. The woman was city council member Sherry Hanson. When word had reached city hall of the third killing of a KRED staffer, she had insisted on sitting in on the meeting. Marvia and Yamura did not want her, but Hanson had gone directly to the chief's office, and she'd been allowed to attend.

The others in the room included Sergeant Abe Craigie and a couple of patrol officers who had worked on the case, Dr. Leo Golden from the coroner's officer, Laura Kern from the evidence lab, Assistant DA Angelina Tesla, a female sergeant from Juvenile Bureau, and a civilian from Berkeley Mental Health.

Marvia breathed deeply and opened the meeting. 'We're here to review the case, survey the suspects, get your help and your ideas. This is a messy situation. Three homicides, involvement of narcotics, weapons, juveniles, and possible criminal conspiracy and fraud. So — thanks for coming.'

She reviewed briefly the known facts in

the Bjorner and Mbolo killings. Then she went on to Dayton. 'Since this latest killing is so recent, I'm going to give you some information myself, and then ask Dr. Golden to review the situation from his viewpoint. And I'll ask Sergeant Craigie to fill us in on Dayton.'

Using a different-colored felt marker for each, she turned and wrote the names of the three homicide victims across the top of the whiteboard. In a vertical column at the left of the board, she wrote a list of suspects' names. Her body between the whiteboard and the rest of the room, she listed the suspects, then taped a sheet of butcher paper to the whiteboard to keep the names covered. But she knew where they were; and opposite each suspect's name, beneath each victim's name, she wrote the word MOM all in caps, arranged vertically.

She turned back toward her audience. Simplest approach: run as straight a chronology as she could, allowing for flashbacks and crossovers among the many characters in her story. She consulted her notes and began with the 911 to Dispatch after Radio Red had keeled over in Studio B. She described her work on Bjorner's death, then moved on to her discovery of the body of Sun Mbolo. Then she described her relationship with Lon Dayton. She explained that he had phoned her at the Hall of Justice and told her that he had some materials relevant to the case or cases at hand. She'd gone to his apartment, picked up the materials, and returned to McKinley Avenue. Shortly after that, he'd been killed.

Abe Craigie stood in place and described his role. 'The call came from another tenant of McGee's — female with three small children, living across the hall from the victim. She stated that Dayton often played his old radio shows loudly and kept her children from taking their naps. She said this was the loudest she'd ever heard, and she went to ask Dayton to turn down the volume. She knocked and got no response. She thought maybe he couldn't hear because of the noise, so she rattled the doorknob to get his attention. The door was unlocked. We later confirmed, no sign of forced entry. So we infer the perpetrator was known to the victim.'

The others in the room followed Craigie in different ways. Some took notes; some simply stared. Leo Golden seemed to be ignoring Craigie; he was there to give his report and that was all he cared about. Sherry Hanson simply looked angry.

'When I arrived at the scene,' Craigie continued, 'the reporting person was not present. She had returned to her apartment to phone in her report, and she stayed there to protect her children in case the perpetrator or perpetrators were still in the building. Which he or she or they were not — we canvassed every apartment as well as neighboring buildings. The perp did the job at hand and left.'

Craigie sat down and Dr. Golden got his chance. He took to the spotlight like a Vegas nightclub performer. 'I'm Dr. Leo Golden, deputy coroner, County of Alameda. The coroner himself, Dr. Bisonte, asked me to perform an autopsy on Mr. Dayton. I made it my business to perform this autopsy with the utmost dispatch, even though it meant coming in on my day off. I will not go into full details. I will distribute a handout summarizing my findings, and my full report will be available through the usual channels. For now, I will furnish only the most salient points of my examination of the subject.'

He pulled a small leather notebook from an inside pocket and consulted it. 'Subject was a white male, forty-five years of age. Upon gross examination, subject appears to have been in overall good health for a male of his age. Cause of death was heart failure, caused by an incision of the heart.

'The weapon entered the subject's body, apparently propelled with great force, penetrating the epidermis and the latissimus dorsi, passing beneath the sternum in an upward direction at an angle of approximately forty-five degrees, passing completely through the left ventricle, left atrium, passing behind the main pulmonary artery and entering but not passing completely through the aorta.

Death would have occurred within a matter of seconds of this insult.

'Additionally, I also counted twenty-three puncture wounds to the buttocks: seventeen to the right buttock, six to the left. These were not the cause of death, and a lack of exsanguination indicates that they were administered postmortem. The placement and direction of the punctures would be consistent with their being administered by a right-handed assailant kneeling behind the victim, as the victim lay prone.'

That fit with the Mbolo killing, Marvia thought, nodding.

'One other point of interest,' Golden added. 'As you may be aware, the release of urine and/or fecal matter at the time of death is a common phenomenon. For this reason, as well as the removal of blood or foreign substances, we customarily wash cadavers upon receipt. We do, of course, subject all such materials to separate analysis. In examining the subject, we found irritation and some tearing of the anus. This appears to be the result of attempted anal copulation. However, the irritation and tearing is so slight, we infer that the attempt was unsuccessful. And the absence of anal bleeding indicates that the attempted anal copulation occurred postmortem.' He bowed slightly, and returned to his seat.

Marvia stood up. 'Okay, we're all up to speed, then.' She indicated the white-board using one of the felt-tip markers as a pointer. 'Here are our victims.'

Robert Bjorner . . . Sun Mbolo . . . Lon Dayton.

'And here are our suspects. We're going to eliminate most of them. Whoever is left . . . ' She turned her back to the room and peeled the tape away. There was a gasp when she stood aside, but she waited pointedly, her back to the room.

Robert Bjorner, aka 'Radio Red'
    Bjorner
Sun Mbolo
Herbert Bjorner
Maude Markham
Solomon San Remo
Sherry Hanson
Leon Beiderbecke, aka Little Bix
Naomi Horowitz, aka Margarita

Horowitz, Sojourner Strength
Susan Gerber
Eisako Fuji
Sachiko Fuji
Hiroshi Kojima
Yaeko Kato
Stephen Insetta, aka Blue Beetle
Alice Gonser, aka Acid Alice

There was a gasp, a moment of shocked silence, and then an angry exclamation.

'How dare you!' Council member Sherry Hanson stood with her fists raised. 'How dare you accuse *me* of these crimes! I am an elected member of the city council, and I'm here in my official capacity to find out what's wrong with this police department; why you can't stop a series of murders at a vital civic institution like KRED.'

Marvia kept a straight face.

'Now I know what's wrong,' Hanson continued. She turned, scanning the room. When she spotted Dorothy Yamura she said, 'Lieutenant, I want this woman off the force. At once! And I intend to prefer charges against her for dereliction of duty and disrespect of the city council.'

To Hanson, Yamura said, 'This is an internal police department meeting, Ms. Hanson. I was under the impression you asked to attend, and it was the chief's decision to let you in.'

'What does that mean, Lieutenant?'

'Sergeant Plum is conducting this meeting. She's a highly qualified homicide detective. Do you think we could hear what she has to say?'

'No, we could not! I will not stand here and be vilified by this — this upstart *copper*.'

Yamura said, 'Sergeant Plum, please proceed.'

Marvia did so, watching as Hanson sat angrily back down. 'We will start with the first homicide: that of Robert Bjorner, a.k.a. Radio Red.' She placed three cardboard diagrams in the whiteboard tray. One was a sketch of the Barbara Jordan Boulevard establishments — KRED, Amazon Rain Forest, Bara Miyako, Bix's Wax Cylinder — and of the KRED parking area and Shaughnessy's Saloon around the corner on Huntington Way. The second was a sketch of the KRED/Oceana building layout. The third was a sketch of Studio B — the furniture, door, heavy glass window, microphones, and the body of Robert Bjorner.

'Now, let's test each suspect for means, opportunity, and motive for committing the crime. First on our list is Robert Bjorner himself. Could this have been a suicide?' She pointed at the letters 'MOM' at the intersection of Robert Bjorner and Robert Bjorner. 'Method? Poison. That's no problem. He carried his meal with him into Studio B, against station policy. And before eating, he lit up a joint, also against policy.' She made a check mark on the whiteboard. 'Opportunity? More of the same, eh?' No one objected. She made another check mark.

'But motive is a big problem. Why would Radio Red kill himself? He was being squeezed out of KRED, but his history is that of a scrapper. He wouldn't have taken the coward's way out. And the scripts of his final week's broadcasts were all typed up, all ready to be used. He went to the studio, script in hand. I can't believe he meant to kill himself.'

There was no disagreement to that. She made an X opposite the second M, and drew a line through Robert Bjorner's name.

'Our next suspect is Sun Mbolo, station manager of KRED.'

Somebody called out, 'She was the next victim, so why is she a suspect?'

While the meeting was in progress, council member Hanson stomped from the room and slammed the door behind her.

'There were three murders,' Marvia answered the questioner. 'The second and third were committed in similar fashion, and it looks as if they were committed by the same perp. But the first was committed by a completely different method. Isn't it possible that Sun Mbolo — or Lon Dayton — was responsible for the Bjorner killing, and that someone else then killed Mbolo and Dayton? Not saying it's so, just that it could be.'

That drew agreement.

'All right. The method of killing was poison. An amazing stew of poisonous seafood, in fact, served up in a Bara Miyako restaurant carton.'

Someone called out: 'How did it get into Studio B?'

'Easy. The victim carried it in with him. He was paranoid. He arrived early at the studio with his script and his meal and some interesting drugs. Mostly cannabis, and not enough hard to be serious, but an amazing cocktail nonetheless. He carried a small portable device and locked the studio door from the inside. There was no other way in or out of Studio B.'

Somewhere in the distance, Marvia heard shouting. That would be council member Hanson in the chief's office.

'Why would he eat half a container of poisoned food?' someone asked.

Laura Kern answered that one. 'It was heavily seasoned with hot spices. He wouldn't have known until it was too late.'

'And he was nearly blind,' Marvia added. 'He couldn't have seen that the food looked wrong. The question of method doesn't preclude Ms. Mbolo.' She put a check mark beside the first M opposite Mbolo's name.

Opportunity was not so easy. Where and how had Mbolo got the poisoned meal, and how had she got it into Bjorner's possession? And motive was even worse. Mbolo must have had an inkling that Radio Red was going to end his radio career with a bang not a whimper, and she might have preferred Bjorner not delivering those broadcasts. But there was nothing in the scripts seriously damaging to Mbolo, and even if there had been, she would not have known any of the details. KRED didn't have a prior-approval policy for its broadcasters' scripts.

'I think you can cross her off. Maybe with a faint line.' A small ripple of laughter greeted Dorothy Yamura's suggestion. 'And besides,' Yamura added, 'I don't like the idea of independent murders that are so connected.'

Herb Bjorner next. Means unchanged, opportunity easy, motive — ah, motive was a problem. For the most part a passive man, content to live in his big house and, when he went out, to drive his big car. Perhaps having Bob Bjorner with him was an inconvenience. How much did Herb value his privacy, and how much had that been impacted by Bob moving into the house after his partner Anitra Colón's death? It seemed very unlikely, and when it came to the killing of Sun Mbolo, even more unlikely, and when it came to the killing of Lon Dayton, it was utterly absurd. Strike Herb Bjorner.

Maude Markham? An interesting notion, if this were one of those old-fashioned puzzlers where the least likely suspect turned out to be the killer. But this was a real-world case, and Markham just didn't fit. A recent arrival in Berkeley, she seemed happy to find a new role in a new community. She had no prior relationship with any of the victims. Opportunity and method might be present, but she simply had no motive.

Solomon San Remo. Connected with the case, yes. Part of the ugly, compli-cated KRED nexus, yes. Could he have run the murderous scenario from his cell at San Quentin? Very far-fetched; and besides, he was busy accumulating brownie points, staying out of trouble and lobbying for his parole. Strike San Remo.

Sherry Hanson. 'Let's save Ms. Hanson for later,' Marvia suggested. 'She may yet return, eh? And I wouldn't want her to accuse us of talking behind her back.'

Leon Beiderbecke. Marvia asked Mack Stillman to talk about this suspect.

'Mr. Beiderbecke runs a record shop on Barbara Jordan Boulevard and he has a disc-jockey show on KRED,' Stillman began. He filled in the group on Beiderbecke's arrest and his agreement to assist the SIB. 'He was tied in with a very troubling drug situation that we have under investigation right now. I notice two names on Sergeant Plum's list — Mr. Insetta and Ms. Gonser — that are familiar to me. Plus of course Mr. San Remo, but I've dealt with Sanctimonious Solly before and I'll deal with him again if I have to. It looks as if there's a good deal of recreational drug use at KRED, but we're not going to get all in an uproar if consenting adults want to smoke some weed. You all know the city policy on that. It's the crackheads and speed-freaks who cause most of our trouble.

'I'm much more concerned with Insetta and Gonser's activities in selling to kids, starting with grass and then escalating right up to paraphernalia, hard stuff, and weapons. That's what we're pursuing, in cooperation with the Juvenile Bureau. As for Beiderbecke — I don't know the situation at KRED — that's Homicide's concern; but as far as I can see, there's no reason to consider Mr. Beiderbecke a suspect.'

Marvia thanked Stillman. 'In short,' she summarized, 'regarding the Bjorner one eighty-seven, I think Beiderbecke might have had motive, but only a very weak one. There was an arts-versus-politics struggle going on at KRED, and Beiderbecke was on the arts side and Bjorner was on the politics side, but neither was a leading player. I'll concede that Beiderbecke could have been involved in Bjorner's death, but he's very much a long shot. And he certainly had no reason to go after Mbolo or Dayton. So — are we agreed? — let's cross him off.'

In the silence of the briefing room, she thought she heard Sherry Hanson's voice, shriller and louder than she'd ever heard it before. And the rumble of the chief's voice. Marvia continued with her work.

Naomi Horowitz and Susan Gerber. Horowitz was another KRED old-timer. Marvia explained that she'd worked at the station years before, and taken a long leave of absence following the injury that left her a quadriplegic. There was no way she could have murdered Radio Red — alone. But with the assistance of Susan Gerber, everything changed. They even had access to exotic sea creatures. Marvia had seen Gerber working at an aquarium tank in the back of Amazon Rain Forest. She would have contact with importers and suppliers of exotic fishes, maybe even including blue-ringed octopus and puffer-fish. And shellfish contaminated with *gonyaulax* would be harder to avoid than to obtain.

But again, there was no motive. Horowitz was on the same side as Bjorner, and Gerber was only concerned with the welfare of her partner, not the internal squabbles of the radio station. If Horowitz's own radio show had been in danger of cancellation — the one she conducted in her Sojourner Strength persona — then there might have been a reason to kill Sun Mbolo. But no reason to kill the inoffensive, non-threatening Lon Dayton. One out of three was not good enough. Cross off Horowitz and Gerber.

And cross off Mr. and Mrs. Fuji. There was simply nothing there to connect them with the victims. Radio Red had been a sometime customer at their restaurant, and that was, if anything, reason to want him alive, not dead.

Hiroshi Kojima and Yaeko Kato. Another pair, this time grandfather and granddaughter. Neither Kojima nor Kato looked like a viable suspect. Kojima could have prepared the fatal seafood stew. He certainly had the skills — he ran the kitchen at Bara Miyako; and when the order was received for Robert Bjorner's last meal, he could have substituted the blue-ringed octopus, pufferfish, and contaminated shellfish for the benign ingredients that should have gone into the container. But someone had to tell him that this order was for Bjorner. Furthermore, those deadly fishes would not be kept in the kitchen of a restaurant. Someone had to make a special run to get them, and not just to the fish market, either. They would have to come from someplace where aquatic creatures were kept for other purposes than as the stuff of gourmets' pleasure. Someplace like a shop that offered rare and exotic biological specimens for researchers or hobbyists. Someplace like the Amazon Rain Forest. And that brought the spotlight back to Horowitz and Gerber.

But there was more. If Kojima was the murderer and Yaeko Kato his accomplice, there still had to be a motive. Radio Red had been an infantryman with the United States Marine Corps on Tarawa, and Hiroshi Kojima had been a cook with the Japanese Imperial Marines on that same island. During that same battle, Bjorner's eyes had been severely damaged by burning white phosphorus, and Kojima's had been ruined. The Imperial Marines had been ordered to fight and die to the last man, but Kojima's blinding had resulted in his being taken prisoner instead. Shame! He had lived with his shame for more than fifty years. Had he expunged his shame, in his own mind, by killing Robert Bjorner? Was there a statute of limitations on revenge? Was there a rationality to vengeance?

For Bjorner's death, the combination of Kojima and Kato scored check marks for method, opportunity, and motive. But for Mbolo's death, and for Dayton's — nothing.

A sergeant from the Juvenile Bureau raised her hand. 'I'm sorry. That ice-pick — I can't get that out of my mind. What kind of monster — '

'Right.' Marvia knew this young woman. She had a background in social work, and was still more social worker than cop. She'd toughen up or she'd get out of the PD and go to work for somebody like Berkeley Mental Health. In fact, she was sitting next to a mental health worker right now. The shrink leaned over and whispered something to the Juvenile Bureau sergeant.

'Please,' Marvia said, 'stand up. Introduce yourself and share that with us.'

The shrink stood, blushing. 'I'm, uh, Kelly Hernandez. The ice-pick there is a clear sign of hostility. In both of the attack killings, the knife was the murder weapon. In both cases, there is evidence of tearing, genital or anal. But in neither case is there evidence of penetration or ejaculation.'

A door slammed loudly. Hernandez resumed. 'The attacker's conduct indicates severe sexual problems — dysfunction, impotence, necrophilia. When he was unable to perform, even with a cadaver for a partner, he took out his rage by stabbing his, ah, failed sexual object with the ice-pick. Again, think of his success — as killer — with the big-bladed kitchen knife. This is followed by his failure to perform with his own sexual organ, followed by the angry — or petulant — attacks with the ice-pick.' She lowered herself halfway into her seat, then pushed herself upright again. 'There was one other thing. The, um, undergarments. Shorts, panties, whatever.'

Marvia nodded encouragement. 'We couldn't find Mbolo's or Dayton's. Mbolo was wearing a dress, which was pulled up around her waist. Dayton was wearing pants, pulled down around his knees.'

'Yes.' Hernandez waved both her hands. 'The fatal wound, delivered in Mbolo's case from behind, in Dayton's from in front. The attempted rape. The failure. The rage. His hand stabbing the woman's breast, the man's buttocks. Finally, the symbolic success — the ice-pick penetrating the victim's anus.'

The young officer from Juvenile Bureau looked sick.

'As for the underwear — he took Mbolo's panties as a way of stealing her vagina. He took Dayton's drawers, too. But he couldn't get them past Dayton's pants, and he was too hurried to remove the pants first. Or too excited. So he used his big knife to cut away the drawers. Hence the two smears of blood that were described for us. When you find the killer, you will find an impotent bisexual male with Sun Mbolo's and Lon Dayton's underpants in his possession, and Dayton's will have been slashed.' She sat down.

For the first time in her career, Marvia Plum was present when a room full of cops burst into applause during a brainstorming session. Kelly Hernandez lowered her head.

Back to business. Did Steve Insetta and/or Alice Gonser have any motive for killing Bob Bjorner? Only if they believed he was planning to blow the whistle on the drug scene at KRED. Insetta and Gonser were one-time functionaries in Solomon San Remo's empire. With Insetta's departure for San Quentin, they had inherited a prosperous and growing business, and they had no intention of being outed on the air by one of their own customers.

Radio Red was himself a user. Why would he reveal the situation at KRED? Answer: Bjorner belonged to the 'do as I say, not as I do' school of morality.

Insetta was Radio Red's buddy. He was the classic hanger-on. Every institution had them, and serving as a drug supplier was a highly favored way of attaching yourself to a rock band, or a motorcycle gang — or a radio station. Insetta, or possibly Gonser acting for him, could have got the poisoned seafood from Amazon Rain Forest and given it to Radio Red. It might have looked odd, but with Bjorner's very bad eyes, he wouldn't have seen that. And with the heavy spices in the container, he wouldn't have noticed that the flavor was off until it was too late.

Insetta would have driven the stolen van to Sun Mbolo's house in the hills and parked it while he committed the second murder. Or Alice Gonser might have driven the van around the streets and picked Insetta up after he was finished.

Means and opportunity were no problem, but motive was. Except that Mbolo was in the vanguard of a new clean-and-sober regime at KRED. The loss of customers that represented might be a minor blow to Insetta's business, but a thorough housecleaning at KRED would inevitably have led to him, and he had no interest in facing trial for his illegal business. Further, by that time, he had killed Bjorner. In for a shilling, in for a pound!

And as for Lon Dayton, that was the final piece in the puzzle. Dayton didn't seem to be a drug user. All else aside, he couldn't afford it; what little disposable income he had went into blank cassettes and audio equipment. But Insetta's unofficial insider status at KRED meant that he knew everything that was going on there. He knew about Dayton's immense audio archive. He knew that the Berkeley Police Department's investigation was closing in on him. And he either knew or suspected that Dayton would have the old tapes that would bring KRED's ancient skeletons rattling out of the closet, bring spotlights glaring down on the station and on him, and leave him on a spot he couldn't get off.

Insetta wasn't involved with the simmering tax scandal, but . . . At this point Marvia had to provide a broad-brush description of that persistent mess. But Solomon San Remo had been deeply involved, and if anyone followed the trail to Solly — as Marvia had done — then Insetta was imperiled as well.

The sexual attacks on Mbolo and Dayton were incidental. Insetta went to each of their homes to kill them, and to Dayton's home to find and steal the old Radio Red tape about the San Remo/Austen Theater tax scam. Once he'd killed Mbolo and Dayton, Insetta tried to have his jollies with them, and failed both times, and took out his frustration and anger with the ice-pick attacks.

'Wait a minute.' Angelina Tesla, pinstriped and high-heeled, raised her hand. 'What about that crazy fax? And while we're at it, are Insetta and what's-her-name, Gonser, still hanging around Berkeley? If I were them, I'd be long gone by now. Who needs to start killing people when you can just pack up and go away?'

'Okay, first the fax.' Marvia found the photocopy of the message and read it: 'Three hours murderer stay quite no speke brethe speke no brethe.'

'What's that about?' Tesla asked.

Marvia dropped the sheet of paper. 'I think Steve Insetta knew that Hiroshi Kojima had a motive for killing Radio Red. I think the fax — he could have sent it from anywhere, even from an ordinary desktop computer if it was connected to a telephone line — was designed to send us off, looking for a killer whose English was very limited to say the least. Of all the people on our suspect list — and Insetta, brainy fellow, could just as easily have made his own version — Mr. Kojima would be the obvious lead to pursue. But when we did our canvass, and when I followed it up at Bara Miyako, I talked only to Mr. and Mrs. Fuji. At first. And they didn't hold my interest. I only found Mr. Kojima later, and by then it was too late for Insetta to nudge me onto him. Not with Sun Mbolo already dead.'

Tesla was satisfied about the fax. But what about her second question?

Marvia nodded. 'I don't think this case is unique, but I've met more odd types . . . Look, everybody lives in her own world, don't you think?' Tesla nodded.

'Bob Bjorner was still fighting the cold war. Sun Mbolo was trying to put Ethiopia behind her and become a one-hundred-percent American. Lon Dayton was living in those thrilling days of yester-year with his cowboys and his spacemen and what all else. Insetta and Gonser came back from South America preaching the gospel of salvation through drugs. They were — they *are* — totally absorbed in what they're doing. They were probably sincere and decent people when they started.' She shrugged. 'Maybe not. I don't know. But they fried their brains, that's for sure. They're intelligent, but they can't see beyond their immediate situation. They might pack up and go at any time, but they haven't so far because they're having such a groovy time where they are.'

Lieutenant Yamura spoke. 'You've already asked for a warrant for Insetta and Gonser, Sergeant Plum?'

'I have.'

A uniformed officer cleared his throat and raised his hand. Marvia recognized the man, a veteran she had long respected. 'That warrant,' he began when she nodded to him. 'On what charge? You didn't just put their names on a list and eliminate everybody else, did you?'

'I've got three signed statements, one from a suspect we turned and two from juveniles. Actually the juveniles' are stronger — they actually made buys from Insetta and Gonser, and they eyeballed firearms sales to minors. Mack Stillman is in on it.'

Stillman grunted. 'I'm out to put my homicides on these two skells, but at the very least we can lock 'em up on the other charges.'

'Okay,' Marvia said. 'Go get the bad guys, that's my motto.'

'Right.' Dorothy Yamura stood up and nodded toward Marvia. 'Then let's move.'

But before they could, the door swung open and the chief of police strode into the room, followed by the furious council member Sherry Hanson.

Assistant District Attorney Angelina Tesla stood up. With three long-legged strides, she stood nose to nose with the newcomers. 'Ms. Hanson, I have some good news for you. I've heard Sergeant Plum's presentation, and I can assure you that you have been eliminated as a suspect in the three homicides.'

Hanson shot a triumphant glance at the chief.

'And I have some bad news,' Tesla resumed. 'I'm going to recommend to my boss that we reopen the Austen Theater tax issue. Something was not right there, and I'm afraid that you're deeply involved.'

Hanson growled.

Tesla said, 'I'd suggest that you get hold of your lawyer right away. In the meanwhile, I'd appreciate it if you remain here in the Hall of Justice while I get back to the courthouse and apply for an order sealing your office and its contents.'

22

Marvia sat with a few other parents and friends, watching the scrimmage game: Benjamin Banneker Junior High School versus Emiliano Zapata Academy. The game was only for practice — official play would begin next week — but the kids were playing hard. This was their last warm-up game, and the starting lineup for the regular season was still fluid. Ed Florio, doubling as baseball coach, was pretty confident of his team, which included Hakeem White and Jamie Wilkerson.

Marvia looked about her. The turnout was sparse. Moms and dads were at work. Among the scattered adults, she recognized Tanya Johnson's parents and their younger son, Tanya's little brother. Tanya had had an older brother who played center field. The parents were trying gamely to keep their sons on an even keel after their sister's death. Ibrahim White was at work, but Yasmina was there in her Muslim scarf, cheering for Hakeem.

Marvia looked toward the main exit from the field. A tall cyclone fence surrounded the grassy area, and a few spectators leaned or sat against it. Marvia studied a man in a watch cap, a dark-colored sweatshirt, and olive-colored army fatigue pants. He stood against the fence with a slim woman in a soiled off-white dress. When the man looked straight ahead, Marvia thought she recognized him from the photo Mack Stillman had shown her. He reached into a pocket on his pants and pulled out a white cloth. Then he removed his watch cap, wiped his face and neck with the cloth, and replaced the cap and shoved the cloth back in his pocket. When he turned to talk with his companion, Marvia could see the large blue insect tattooed beside his far eye.

Mom Marvia tried to keep her mind on her son and the game while Cop Marvia surveyed the spectators. She counted several officers beside herself in the stands or on the field. Homicide and

Narcotics had each contributed a couple.

Neither Yamura nor Stillman would want to make the bust during a baseball game with dozens of kids on the field and a scattering of spectators looking on. There was too much potential for harm to an innocent bystander. A shoot-out between cops and thugs with a stray shot taking down a third party was every cop's nightmare.

Marvia scanned the field again. She saw a youngster approach Steve Insetta. Something went on between the two, and the youngster handed something to Insetta. Alice Gonser had separated herself from Insetta by ten or fifteen yards. The youngster walked to Gonser and pointed back toward Insetta. Blue Beetle nodded. Acid Alice put her hand to her mouth, then held it to the youngster's mouth. The youngster headed toward the street.

Marvia watched the kid moving away. The moment he was out of Insetta and Gonser's sight, Marvia knew, he'd be picked up by a cop.

Ed Florio had trotted to the pitcher's

mound, calling the catcher from behind the plate. After a brief conference, the catcher returned to his position and Florio to the bench.

The batter swung, sending a hot grounder back up the middle. Hakeem snatched the ball at belt-buckle level and shoveled it to Jamie, who scraped his toe on the bag at second and threw straight and true to his teammate at first base. The Clockers girls and parents in the bleachers cheered. The Zapatista fans moaned. Ed Florio and the players from the Clocker bench poured onto the field to congratulate their teammates.

Marvia Plum had started onto the field to hug her son when she heard the shouting. Three SIB officers had closed in on Steve Insetta and Alice Gonser. Whatever Yamura and Stillman's plan had been, Beetle and Alice had done something to provoke the officers. The trap was sprung.

Marvia swerved toward the scene, plowing through fans as she went. The officers were shouting at Insetta and Gonser, who were running toward the opening in the cyclone fence. A black-and-white, siren screaming, lurched to the curb, and a uniformed officer leaped out. Two other black-and-whites screeched to a halt.

Insetta and Gonser angled away from the gate, then toward the main school building. If they could get inside, they might be able to make their way out the far end of the building and reach an alley that would lead them into a warren of driveways and backyards.

A door opened in the school building and a uniformed officer appeared. Insetta and Gonser were close to the building. Gonser turned toward Insetta. He drew his arm back and hit her across the face. She crashed to the ground at the uniformed officer's feet while Insetta swerved again, cutting away from the school building and back toward the baseball field.

Most of the players and their families were standing on the infield, staring at the action. A few, anticipating gunplay, had thrown themselves to the ground. The officer at the school door had handcuffed

Alice Gonser and was speaking into his radio. Another uniform had blocked the gate in the cyclone fence. The rest were pursuing Steve Insetta.

The civilians who had dotted the diamond after game's end were scrambling to safety, but many of them were still on the field. Insetta scurried past first base and scampered toward second in a crazy, unintentional parody of a base runner. Ed Florio grabbed Jamie and Hakeem, one with either arm, and yanked them out of Insetta's path, but Jamie twisted out of Florio's grip and threw himself bodily at Insetta. He struck Insetta with his shoulder. His Clockers baseball cap flew off and rolled away.

For a moment Insetta looked startled. Staggering, he grabbed Jamie with his left hand. He doubled over, then rose again with his trademark weapon, a broad-bladed kitchen knife that he'd drawn from his boot. Jamie's hair was too short to offer a good grip, so Insetta yanked him against his body. Jamie's head was pulled tight against Insetta's quilted jacket just at the level of his bottom rib.

Marvia drew her S&W Airweight and planted her feet. She held the revolver in both hands, her left elbow braced against her hip the way she'd practiced for years. She yelled at Insetta: 'Drop the weapon. Drop the weapon and let the boy go.' She could hear voices from around her, but they were millions of miles away, as real as the whispers of interstellar radio voices in the night. She couldn't understand them. Her peripheral vision narrowed until there was nothing left in the world except the Blue Beetle and her son. She yelled again at Insetta.

He said: 'This little bastard did it. He — '

Jamie's life was at stake. If Marvia fired . . . If she didn't fire . . .

She squeezed off a round that smashed Insetta's face into a dark red explosion. He toppled backward, his arms outflung, the knife tumbling in one direction and Jamie staggering in the other. Marvia ran forward with her weapon in her hand. Insetta couldn't be alive, but somehow he was, and he was scrabbling at his other boot. He brought his hand back up and sunlight glinted off the point of his ice-pick. Marvia fired into the center of Insetta's chest and hot blood spattered her hands and face.

The world closed down to a tight compartment containing nothing but Marvia Plum and the bloody corpse of Steve Insetta. The tip of a white cloth protruded from his fatigue pants pocket. She bent for a closer look: the cloth was stained with reddish-brown streaks. She held her Airweight in her right hand and plucked at the cloth with her left. The cloth came the rest of the way out of Insetta's pocket. Marvia dropped it to the ground. It was a torn and bloodstained pair of men's under-drawers. Something made her reach into the pocket. This time she pulled out a pair of women's panties.

She fell to her knees beside the body, every nerve in her system quivering. Then she scanned the area around her again, looking for danger, but saw none. She put her fingertips on the side of Insetta's throat, searching for a pulse she knew would not be there. A hand fell gently on her shoulder and she looked up to see a familiar uniformed officer, the veteran who'd asked about the arrest warrant.

He said, 'Bozo here is evidence now, Sergeant. That's all he is.' He held out a strong hand and helped her to her feet.

★   ★   ★

Sleep was hopeless. Marvia was sweating. She threw off the covers and began to shiver. When she pulled up a sheet, she found it wet with perspiration.

She'd already spent an hour with the shrink and another with IA, and they'd sent her home and said they'd both see her again tomorrow.

She twisted the tuning knob on her radio and found KRED. Whoever was in charge was rerunning an old Lon Dayton show. Courageous but dim-witted Nick Train and beautiful Tina Carter and wicked Elsie Desmond were embroiled in a fresh crisis.

Poor Lon Dayton. Bob Bjorner, Radio Red, hadn't been the heart and soul of KRED after all. Sojourner Strength had been wrong. It was Lon Dayton who deserved her praise. Poor, half-crazed, well-intentioned Lon Dayton, the King of Old-Time Radio, the Master of Time and Space, the Lord of Laughter and Tears. The heart and soul of KRED.

The Electro Super Bomber rose roaring from the jungle of Oaxaca with Wright Martin at its controls and Nick Train and Tina Carter and the Russian emissary, Vladimir Borofsky, sharing crew quarters for the flight back to the U.S. Little did they know that an experimental Nazi rocket weapon was arching through the stratosphere, headed straight for their plane . . .

KRED had been a community asset after all, but it was no vanguard of some vainglorious revolution. It was a home for life's casualties, a refuge for the dispossessed, a place where Berkeley's losers could scrape together a little self-respect for a few minutes once a week. But that KRED was breathing its last, with the final broadcast of *Lon Dayton's Old-Time Radio Heaven*.

Marvia turned off the radio and climbed out of bed. She crossed the room and switched on the student lamp that had stood on her desk since she was Jamie's age. She sat at her desk, barefoot and pajama-clad, and turned and peered out the window into the dark night. In the tree-house in the California blue oak, the ghost of her father grinned proudly at the ghost of his daughter as a child. She felt a lump in her throat and tried to make the ghosts stay there, but they disappeared before her eyes.

She opened her desk drawer and took out a piece of stationery that had been in the desk as long as the lamp had stood on it. Then she uncapped the pen that wrote with real ink, that Jamie had given her for Mother's Day three years ago.

She wrote like a woman in a trance. No date, no salutation, just her letter.

Damn you, Lindsey. You don't understand women. You never did. We're different creatures. You don't know what I think. You don't know what I feel.

What can I say? Would it help if I said I hate you?

Knock on my door. Ring the bell. Please.

At least we can try.

She signed the letter and folded it carefully and sealed it in an envelope. She wrote the last address she had for him on the envelope. His Denver address. The only stamp she could find was a silly *Love* stamp with a picture of a puppy on it and a big red heart; she fixed it to the envelope.

She walked downstairs and sat for a while in the darkened kitchen. Then she stood up and went to the gas stove. She turned on a burner and destroyed the letter.

She returned to the table and sat in the old wooden chair, in the darkness.

$$\star \quad \star \quad \star$$

Good night, sweet prince, and flights of angels sing thee to thy rest.

The voice was Jessie Loman's, but the delivery had none of the hesitation and uncertainty of the heavyset, bespectacled receptionist in the lobby of KRED. Loman's voice was transformed. It was silky smooth, huskily sensuous, seductive, and yet tragic.

The time is out of joint, O cursed spite, that ever thou wast born to set it right.

Had they been lovers? Two lost souls touching in the dream world of radio?

'This is KRED's new feature, *Jessie Loman's Radio Heaven*, now and forever dedicated to Lon Dayton, the King of OTR, the Master of Time and Space, the Lord of Laughter and Tears. Tonight we heard the very first installment of *Nick Train, Crime Fighter*. Nick Train was Lon's favorite series, and I can't help thinking, sitting alone here in the KRED studio, playing the old, old show, that Lon can hear me . . . wherever he is.'

Marvia Plum sat up in her bed and turned up the volume on her radio.

'And so, this is Jessie Loman, signing off for now. We'll be back tomorrow night, same time, same station. Good night, Lon. Good night, my darling man. *The rest is silence.*'

We do hope that you have enjoyed reading this large print book.

Did you know that all of our titles are available for purchase?

We publish a wide range of high quality large print books including:

Romances, Mysteries, Classics
General Fiction
Non Fiction and Westerns

Special interest titles available in large print are:

The Little Oxford Dictionary
Music Book, Song Book
Hymn Book, Service Book

Also available from us courtesy of Oxford University Press:

Young Readers' Dictionary
(large print edition)
Young Readers' Thesaurus
(large print edition)

For further information or a free brochure, please contact us at:
Ulverscroft Large Print Books Ltd.,
The Green, Bradgate Road, Anstey,
Leicester, LE7 7FU, England.
Tel: (00 44) **0116 236 4325**
Fax: (00 44) **0116 234 0205**

Other titles in the
Linford Mystery Library:

A PLAGUE OF SPIES

Michael Kurland

A group of international spies has assembled in the small nation of Alba. Interpol guesses that they aren't there for their holidays — but has no clue as to the real plans being set in motion. Peter Carthage, WAR, Inc.'s slickest agent, is sent to infiltrate and destroy — and ends up captured by an order of most peculiar monks. As Carthage learns the sinister secret of the monastery, he finds himself in the middle of the greatest coup in the history of crime . . .

A MIDWIFE'S CHRISTMAS

Catriona McCuaig

Midwife Maudie and Detective Sergeant Dick Bryant are settling into parenthood, preparing for baby Charlie's first Christmas. But this December will prove to be one of the most eventful in memory. An unknown assailant is attacking multiple Father Christmases. A vulnerable young girl is missing, thrown out by her father in disgrace. And Dick's patience with Maudie's interference in police cases is wearing thin. Meanwhile, there are the politics of the village nativity play to contend with — from protecting soloists' fragile egos to wrangling live farmyard animals. Then a shocking event puts Charlie in danger . . .

THE SILVER CHARIOT KILLER

Richard A. Lupoff

It's Christmas week in New York, and the frozen body of Cletus Berry, Hobart Lindsey's partner, has been found in a back alley alongside that of a known criminal. Was there a connection between the two men? This wouldn't normally be Lindsey's case, but when a man's partner is killed, he must do something about it. Now separated from Marvia Plum, Lindsey is on his own, and the body count is set to rise unless he can solve the mystery of the Silver Chariot . . .

MALICE IN WONDERLAND

Rufus King

Three tales of mystery and the macabre. When the body of a woman clothed in the scantiest of swimsuits is found lying close to the surf on the private beach of a motel, Florida Police Chief Bill Duggan faces a baffling problem. Did she accidentally drown, or commit suicide? Or has she been murdered by one of the very strange guests at the motel? In other stories, a small girl's talent in witchcraft unmasks a killer, and a man's fourth marriage has a fatal ending.